Black Eden Publications Presents...

Counterfeit

Dreams 3

A Dream's Nightmare

www.SashaRavae.com

BLACK EDEN PUBLICATIONS™

Counterfeit *Dreams 3*

ISBN: 978-1511623469

10 9 8 7 6 5 4 3 2 1

Printed in the United States

Counterfeit

Dreams 3

A Dream's Nightmare

Chapter 1

Reagan paced around her lonely room with her eyes glued to her cellphone that sat on the night stand next to her. "He's never late," she said out loud, "Maybe he got caught up. He could just be busy."

She needed to reassure herself, but Jewel's absence was sometimes too much for her to handle. It had been six months since he had been in jail, but he made it a point to call her every night, and he was never late.

"Did Dad call yet?" Jailen asked walking sleeplessly into the room. Reagan usually let him stay up late to speak to Jewel. Even though he was gone, she needed him to still be there for his family.

"Not yet, J, but he's gonna call. He always calls. You know that. Now go finish watching TV," she said looking into the face of Jewel's younger self.

Suddenly feeling nauseous, she sat down. She was beginning the last trimester of her pregnancy, and she wanted nothing more than for it to be finally over. She was miserable. Before Jewel was arrested, Reagan had the scare of her life. While waiting for him to come home, she started bleeding. Home alone with Jailen, she waited for as long as she could for Jewel, but she was scared of losing her baby. Without thinking twice, she grabbed Jailen and took herself to the hospital. When she arrived the doctors reassured her that she had come in at the right time. If she would have waited, she would've lost the baby. After examining her, the doctor noticed that her cervix was opening, and her body was going into premature labor. Scared and alone, Reagan didn't know what to do. Jewel wasn't answering his phone, so she did the only thing she could think of, and that was to call Jailen's grandmother Paula. Wanting the best for her grandson, she came and picked him up. After making sure Jailen was situated, Reagan continued her search for Jewel. She called his phone over and over again, but he never called back. A day later, she received a call from an unknown number. Stuck in the hospital, she had no other choice but to answer it.

"You have a collect call from the Sacramento County Jail from 'Jewel.' If you wish to accept this call, please press one."

Reagan felt like her prayers had been silently answered. "Baby?" she cried into the phone.

Sasha Ravae

"Listen, Rea, I'm sorry, okay? Some shit went down with Diamond. My court date isn't until Monday, so I'ma be in here for the weekend."

"What happened?"

"We'll talk later," he said not wanting to talk over the phone.

After receiving a call from Diamond, he went to her boyfriend's house to rescue her from herself. Diamond's drug habit had gotten out of control after she started seeing Marcus. She went from smoking weed and taking E pills now and again to snorting powder and heroin more frequently than she could remember. Even though Jewel had made it more than clear to her that their relationship was over, he still loved her, and he would have done whatever it took to protect her.

When Jewel arrived at Marcus' house, he was high as a kite. Jewel knew that Marcus wasn't going to just hand Diamond over to him. He felt like he controlled her, but in reality, she was just a slave to the high, and Marcus was the master providing it. After an altercation with Marcus, Detective Roberts showed up along with his junior detective Vanessa to arrest Jewel. Roberts wanted to charge him, Sacario, and Pop with Brandon and Golden's murders, but without Brandon's body or any other evidence, the DA had nothing to go on. Pop was OR'd that same night. County was too full to keep him in jail for only having a single blunt in his car, and they couldn't find anything else to charge Sacario with, but Marcus was able to press charges against Jewel for trespassing and assault, and Roberts took that opportunity to gather more evidence against the M.A.C. Boys.

Reagan sat in the cold hospital bed as tears continued to roll down her face. The last time she was in a hospital, it was because Styles almost stole her life from her. She wanted to be happy about her pregnancy, but it seemed like nothing ever went right. She felt cursed. She knew she and Jewel were destined to be together, but something was always standing in the way.

"Did you and Jailen make it to the hotel?" Jewel questioned. Even though he was locked up, he had to make sure that they were safe. Kisino wanted Jewel's head and he knew that nothing would be off limits.

"Jewel, I'm in the hospital. They admitted me."

"What happened? Are you okay? Where's Jailen?" he hurried to ask.

Counterfeit *Dreams 3*

"I called Paula to come and get him. The doctors said that my body is going into premature labor, and they want me to be on bed rest. Whatever the fuck that means," Reagan screamed out in frustration. She couldn't imagine herself being stuck in a hospital bed again especially when Jewel needed her. "I called her cause I knew he didn't want to be here. He doesn't even know me." She felt overwhelmed. She didn't know how to help.

"Fuck. Fuck. Fuck," he said slamming the phone into the wall. Reagan meant everything to him, and even though he was having a hard time accepting that she was carrying another man's baby, he wanted to be there for her, but at that moment, he was helpless.

"I'm gonna figure this out, okay, baby?"

"You have thirty more seconds," an automated voice interrupted.

"I gotta go, Rea, but I'ma call you tomorrow, so keep money on your phone. I'll let you know more when I find out."

"Jewel, I'm scared. What am I supposed to do? I have to do something. I can't just stay here. You need me. I'm just gon' let the doctor know that I can't stay. They can't fucking make me," she said making up her mid.

"Baby, listen. I know that you're scared, but I need you to be strong for the both of us. Jailen will be fine. Paula would never let anything happen to him. Trust me. I just need you to rest. Stressing out about me being in here isn't gonna help you or the baby, so try to relax. I'm gonna fix all of this, okay?"

Reagan didn't respond. She wanted to believe in the words that soothed her fears, but she couldn't.

"You believe me, right?"

"Yes."

"I'ma call you tomorrow. Stay by your phone. I love you."

"I love you too…" Before Reagan could finish, the call ended. She spent the rest of the day crying. She had gone so long without Jewel, and she didn't want to have to feel that pain ever again.

The hospital kept Reagan under observation for a few weeks to monitor the progress of the baby. Besides the daily calls from Jewel, she had nothing else to look forward to, so being on bed rest was easier than she thought it would be. Once the doctors felt like she was stable enough, they advised her to continue resting at home until she became full-term if she could wait that long. Reagan was reluctant to go home alone to Jewel's huge house especially since he wanted her to leave Sacramento all together, but she had nowhere else to go. When she got home, the house she had briefly shared with Jewel felt so unfamiliar. Paula was worried about Diamond being in and out of Jailen's life, so a few days later, she made it a point to have him go home. Reagan never mentioned Jewel's whereabouts. He was always inconveniently not there, and Reagan began to run out of excuses, but over the weeks, Diamond had made her presence known more and more distracting Paula from his absence. Diamond begged Paula to let her see Jailen, but Paula would only agree if she went to rehab. Diamond wasn't ready to let go of her lifestyle or Marcus, so the opportunity to be back in her son's life seemed further and further away.

Even though Reagan was advised to rest until she delivered, she had no choice but to hold Jewel down. She had been the problem the entire time in their relationship, so she wanted to finally prove that he could depend on her as much as she had depended on him. She enrolled Jailen in school by the house because Paula was adamant about Diamond not being able to get in contact with him. She only saw a shell of her daughter, and she didn't want to put her grandson through the confusion. She didn't know how to explain to a 9-year old child that his mom was a drug addict. Soon Reagan found a routine with Jailen in Jewel's absence. She knew that she could never take the place of Diamond, and she didn't want to, but Jailen was a part of Jewel, and that meant something to her. She had to do everything in her power to protect him. Being with him day-in and day-out helped to ease her anxieties about her own baby. She fell in love with Jailen. She loved his young and innocent spirit, and despite the circumstances, she was excited about beginning their blended family.

$$$$$

Reagan lay in her empty bed massaging her belly with cocoa butter. She had gained weight, but she was fortunate to not have any stretch marks, and she wanted to keep it like that. Jailen had fallen asleep disappointed that he didn't get to talk to Jewel. Despite what was going on, his son meant the world to him.

Counterfeit *Dreams 3*

Just as Reagan was about to fall asleep, her phone vibrated against the wooden night stand. It was Jewel. Her heart jumped as she answered the phone. "Hello?"

"Hey, baby, did I wake you?"

"You know I was up. What happened?"

"Some niggas got into it earlier today, and they found one of them dead in his cell, so they instantly shut shit down."

"Oh my god, are you okay?"

"I'm good. I ain't have nothing to do with that shit. I would've called you earlier, but it was hella hot." Jewel tried to stay under the radar, but he knew he needed a phone, so he bought a burner for $1,500.

"I'm so ready for all this bullshit to be over."

"Man, who you telling?"

"Have you talked to your lawyer?"

"Yeah, he talking that same shit. They want me to take a deal for the assault charge if they drop the trespassing, but I would have to do a year. I'm good. Like I told that nigga I'm not pleading to shit. Diamond would've died if I wasn't there." Jewel hated that he was still in jail. He couldn't post bail because Marcus had a protective order out on him, and being that his family were valued members of the community, the judge denied his petition. Jewel knew that his crimes were petty, but because of Marcus' family's influence, the DA was trying to hit him with whatever was going to put him away.

"Why don't you call your father?" Reagan asked well aware of Joe's legal background.

"For what? I don't need his help. I'ma get out. They have nothing to hold me."

"But it's been six months."

"I'm not calling him. I made my peace with the situation, Rea. Drop it."

After Gabrielle was shot, Jewel went to the hospital to make sure she was okay. When he saw Joe, he let go of everything he had been holding onto for the past eleven years. Even though he resented Joe for leaving him and his mother to be with another woman and starting a new family, Jewel wasn't the same little boy, and he refused to apologize for the person he had become.

"I'm sorry. I just thought he could help."

"Where's Jailen?" he asked wanting to change the subject.

"He's sleep. I let him stay up til like 11:00 p.m., but he was tired."

"Go wake him up," Jewel instructed. Thinking about his relationship with his own father only reiterated the importance of maintaining his relationship with his own son.

Reagan walked across the hall into Jailen's room with her cellphone in hand. She gently rubbed his back hoping to wake him as she played her part with no complaints. "Jailen, baby, your dad is on the phone. He wants to talk to you. Jailen," she said softly.

He grabbed the phone with his eyes closed still half sleep, "Daddy?"

"Hey, son, I didn't mean to wake you. I just wanted to talk to you before I went to sleep."

"I thought you forgot to call."

"Never that, J," Jewel said letting his son's voice soothe his soul. He was determined to get back home.

"Are you coming home soon?"

"I hope so. I'm working as fast as I can, okay?"

"Okay, love you, Daddy."

"Love you too, Jailen. Now go back to sleep."

Jailen handed Reagan the phone satisfied with the call as he drifted back into his dreams.

"Hold on," she said into the phone, "Good night, Jailen. You want pancakes in the morning?"

"Are you gonna burn them again?" he giggled.

"No, I've been practicing," she said proud of her cooking progress.

"Can we just go to Denny's?"

"Fine, we'll go to Denny's. See you in the morning," she said closing his door behind her. She waited until she was back in her and Jewel's room before she spoke. "Hello?"

"So you've been cooking?"

"I mean I'm trying. Google is definitely my friend."

"Awwww, look at my baby being all motherly." Jewel felt at ease with Jailen being with her. He knew that she would treat him like her own.

"I just feel bad ordering out every night. My mom cooked for me, so I wanna do it too."

"You're gonna be a great mother, you know that?"

Counterfeit *Dreams 3*

"I hope so. I'm scared though."

Jewel was very proud of the woman Reagan was becoming. They had been through a lot in the past two years, and as much as he loved her, he had lost hope that they would be able to be together again, but when Reagan came back into his life, he couldn't pretend anymore with Diamond. His heart belonged to Reagan, and he knew that if he let her get away again, she might not come back. He was still trying to accept that she was pregnant with Brandon's baby, but his love for her transcended her past mistakes. He knew that if they were going to be together, he would have to forgive her. This was their fresh start.

"You know I'ma marry you, right?"

"Jewel, shut up," she said beginning to blush. She would be lying if she said that the thought never crossed her mind. She wanted nothing more than to be his wife, but she needed him to want it too.

"I'm serious. I've been thinking about you, us, and the baby, and I want to do right by you. Brandon's not here to be a father, and no matter what happened, it's in my heart to take care of the baby like he was my own. Brandon did a lot of fucked up shit, but that was my brother. I can't throw ten plus years of our friendship away. In a way, he gave me this life, and I know it doesn't make any sense because at the same time, my life meant nothing to him, but that wasn't my nigga. Something else had him. We thugged it out ever since I was 15. I can't say I'll ever forgive him, but at the same time, I can never forget him either."

"So because of Brandon you want to marry me?"

Reagan had her own demons to deal with. She didn't need to take on Jewel's too. Brandon was a mistake. She hated that she let herself be weak around him. She never lost love for Jewel, but at that time getting attention meant more.

"No, that's not what I'm saying. What I am saying though is that I'm ready to move on with my life. The situation with Diamond and Brandon are those situations. I just don't want to talk about this shit anymore."

"Well, that's hard to do since your son's mother is still around."

"Whatever the case is with her has nothing to do with us, right?"

"I'm just saying."

"Mark my words, baby. We're getting married, but let me get off this phone. I'ma try to call you guys tomorrow. Love you."

Sasha Ravae

"I love you, Jewel. Good night."

Reagan hung up the phone confused. She and Jewel never really talked about marriage, and she didn't want to if he felt obligated, so she pushed the thought out of her head not taking the promise seriously.

$$$$$

"Dad, it's for you," Gabrielle said bringing the house phone to Joe.

After being shot, Gabrielle straightened up her life. At 18, she refocused on school and the opportunities her parents provided her with. She had to reevaluate her life. While she was in the hospital, K-2 never left her side. He knew that he should have been more careful because she was with him, but the only thing that mattered was making a name for himself in the M.A.C. Boys, but throughout it all, he fell in love with Gabrielle, so he stopped hustling and got a job working with Joe. He knew it would be hard to fit in with her family because of his past, but for her, he wanted to try. She wanted that square life, so he tried to fit her mold. She soon realized that she only chased behind Pop because of his notoriety. She had love for him still, but she loved the attention he received more, and since he never acknowledged their relationship anyway, she was the only one pursuing it. She was done with the life. All being a groupie got her was a couple of bags, shoes, and her pussy ran through.

Joe sat in his office going over various case files. "Who is it?" he asked taking off his reading glasses.

"I don't know. Some woman. I'ma see you later, k? Keith is on his way over here to take me to school."

"What time are you coming home?"

"I don't know. I'll call you."

"Gabby, I…"

"I know, Dad, but I need you to relax. It's been six months. I'm fine, okay? Just trust me a little please."

"The last time I did that you ended up in somebody's hospital bed."

"Dad."

"Call me as soon as you make it to school."

"Bye."

Counterfeit *Dreams 3*

Joe was more than overprotective after Gabrielle came home. He blamed himself for her being in the hospital. As much as he wanted to reconnect with Jewel, he didn't want his old life destroying his new one. Joe didn't know his son anymore, and he didn't know if he ever would.

"This is Joe Sanchez."

"Hi, my name is Reagan Taylor, and I'm a friend of your son Jewel."

"Unh huh, how can I help you today Ms. Taylor?"

"I'm calling because Jewel is in jail."

"Okay." Joe's heart sunk. As much as he loved his son, he didn't know how to help him.

"Mr. Sanchez, Jewel has been in County for six months, and he hasn't been charged with anything. His lawyer doesn't know what he's doing. I was just thinking that since you're a lawyer that..."

"That I could just snap my fingers and Jewel would be free. It's good that he has a lawyer. Let him do his job."

"But he needs your help."

"I would rather not get involved. Have a good day," Joe said attempting to end the conversation.

"Mr. Sanchez, with all due respect, don't you think that you owe this to Jewel?"

"Excuse me?"

"Correct me if I'm wrong, but didn't you leave his mother to be with another woman? You left him alone, and he had to figure out how to be a man completely on his own. And now that you have the chance to help your own son, you don't want to be involved?"

Joe remained silent. As much as he wanted to be a part of Jewel's life, it was hard for him to relive his past. He was deeply in love with his wife and family. How could he connect his dark past to his present?

"I'm sorry I even called you, Mr. Sanchez. Jewel was right."

Before Joe could respond, Reagan hung up. She knew that he could help Jewel get out of jail. Jewel had more than enough money to pay for any attorney, but Marcus' family had the right connections, which was making it much more difficult for him. At this point, Marcus had an image to uphold, and Jewel jeopardized his family's good name. His family didn't want a drug scandal to get out. It would hurt Marcus' professional image as well as his father's.

Joe set the cordless phone down on his desk and placed his head in his hands as the room fell silent.

$$$$$

"So what time you get out today?" K-2 asked pulling up to American River College. He knew that Gabrielle was more than capable of driving herself, but he had made a promise to Joe that he would keep her safe. Joe wasn't too happy with her decision to continue a relationship with K-2, but over time, he was able to gain Joe's trust. Joe could tell that he did have his daughter's best interest at heart, so eventually he grew to accept it.

"4:30 p.m.," Gabrielle said fixing her make-up in the car, "If you want, I can get a ride home with Maleya, so you don't have to come all the way back out here."

"Why would I want you to do that?" K-2 enjoyed every minute they spent together, but he was starting to miss his own space.

"I don't know maybe to get from up under my ass for five fucking seconds. You and my dad need to chill. I get it. You guys are scared, but I was walking around fine before all this shit happened. I need some space. Fuck," she said slamming the overhead mirror closed.

"Where's all this coming from?" K-2 acted surprised, but he was relieved that she was the one who said it first.

"I love you, Keith. I really do, but I need a life outside of you, outside of this. I feel like the only reason you're with me now is to be my babysitter. This arrangement you and my dad got ain't cool."

"What arrangement?"

"Don't play with me, Keith."

K-2 knew that he and Gabrielle had been spending a lot of time together, but he didn't know if Kisino and GMB were going to retaliate for KP's death. Even though he didn't bang anymore, he was still well aware of what was going on in the streets. He refused to believe that Kisino could just forget about what happened or that Jewel would let Golden's murder slide. His indiscretions had to be paid back in blood. That's how the game went. Sacario went back to the Bay to be with his family after he was released from jail, and the M.A.C Boys seemed to be far and few in between, but K-2 knew that Kisino was lurking somewhere in the shadows ready to strike. It was only a matter of time, and even though K-2 felt like he had to protect Gabrielle, he valued their relationship, and he wanted to be with her.

"Listen, man, ain't nobody pressing you, baby. You are a grown-ass woman. You're not a prisoner. You're free to come and go as you please, Gabby. If you wanna hang out with Maleya, okay."

"Really? What's the catch?" She was skeptical because in the couple of months they had been together, she and K-2 were never a part.

"No catch. Against popular belief, ma, I got shit to do too. I was just tryna help you out, feel me?"

"Yeah. Yeah. Yeah, I'll call you when I get home," Gabrielle said leaning over to kiss him.

"Yep."

She got out of the champagne Lexus and walked up the stairs that led to her class. As she was walking inside, her phone rang. She didn't recognize the number, but she answered anyway, "Hello?"

"What's up, Gabby?"

"Pop?" It had been six months since she had last seen him. It was like he fell off the face of the Earth. Despite them being done, she still thought that he cared enough about her to at least make sure she was alive.

"Listen, I know it's been a minute, and I'm probably the last person you wanna hear from, but I think we should talk. Can you meet me somewhere?"

"Pop, we have nothing to talk about." Anger still filled her heart. She had spent three years chasing behind him, and he left her to die. Not once did he call or show up to the hospital.

"Please? I'll come to you."

She weighed out her options, but curiosity got the best of her. "I'm at school, but I get out at 4:30 p.m. You can meet me at ARC."

"Okay, I'll text you when I'm on my way."

"Bye." Gabrielle hung up the phone confused by the call. She tried to forget about Pop, but the way they left things made it hard for her to do that. She continued walking to class as she texted her friend Maleya. *Hey, girl, Keith was tripping again, so I'ma just go home with him. I'll hit you though.*

Sasha Ravae

$$$$$

Pop hung up the phone excited that Gabrielle had agreed to meet with him. After he was released from jail, he had to lay low. He knew that it was only a matter of time before he had to deal with Kisino, and with Jewel out of the picture, he had no direction. He let the money get to his head, and even though he didn't pull the trigger himself, he felt responsible for Will and Golden's deaths. He knew nothing would make things right again, but the guilt he lived with every day was beginning to be too much to bear. He needed guidance. He couldn't get in touch with Jewel because he heard that he was in County, but he knew that Gabrielle might be able to get a message through to him.

$$$$$

K-2 drove around Sac aimlessly. Even though he loved Gabrielle, the nine-to-five square life was not for him. Inside he was miserable. He didn't really see Sacario as much as he used to because he was constantly up under Gabrielle or her father. He missed his old life, and he didn't know how much longer he could pretend. Everything that he had given up to be in a relationship with Gabrielle was everything that made him who he was. After a while, he drove back home. He was off from work, and with Gabrielle's new need for freedom, he had to occupy his time on his own. While he was driving, his phone rang. It was Joe.

"She make it?" he quickly asked. As much as he trusted K-2, he always had to double-check.

"Yes, sir, I dropped her off right in front."

"Okay, good, call me when you pick her up."

"No problem."

"You coming over for dinner?" In just a short amount of time, K-2 had become like family. The more time he spent around him, the fonder Joe became.

"They called me into work, so I'ma head in after I get Gabby home."

"Okay, well, don't forget to call me."

Counterfeit *Dreams 3*

"I won't." K-2 was tired of having the responsibility of watching Gabrielle. He had to get away. Without thinking, he got off the exit, and turned around. His soul craved home, so he headed back to the water.

$$$$$

Pop pulled into a parking space in front of Gabrielle's school. He was eager to see her. Even though he didn't know how to love her, he still cared about her. Pop knew that the chance of them getting back to where they used to be was nonexistent, but he was determined to get his life back. After he was arrested, he was put into a small room with no windows for what seemed like hours, but soon he realized the true reason he was being held for so long.

"Well, Mr. Carter, it's funny how we keep running into each other, huh?" Detective Roberts asked.

Pop kept quiet. He had done more than enough to put him away for life, but Roberts had nothing to go on but hearsay.

"We know that you are and have been affiliated with Jewel Sanchez and the M.A.C Boys and some new group of punks by the name of GMB. Can't make up your mind, can you?"

"I never heard of them," Pop said plainly.

"Tough guy, huh?" Roberts asked becoming irritated. He wanted to bust Jewel and the clique, but he had nothing on them. "Listen, Caseem, we know that you run with the M.A.C Boys, and you've been involved with a couple of murders..."

"I want a lawyer." Pop requested hoping to avoid Roberts' continued harassment.

"We were just talking," he said getting up out of his chair, "But if you insist, Caseem, you're free to go. Just know that I'm watching you." At the mention of a lawyer, Roberts knew he had nothing to hold him on. He needed more, and he hoped that Pop would lead him exactly to where he needed to be.

After being released, Pop went home and finished packing the rest of his stuff. He had always prided himself on staying under the radar especially when he started hanging with Jewel. Jewel always taught him that he could have the finer things in life, but he didn't have to let everyone know what those finer things were. After he took Pop under his wing, Pop began to save money because the future became important to him. He didn't just care about how he was going to survive the day.

He packed up his jewelry and clothes and threw them in his trunk. He was ready to leave everything behind him and start over, but he had a few loose ends to take care of first. When Pop arrived at ARC, from the corner of his eye, he saw Gabrielle walking up to the car. Her jet black hair glistened in the sunlight with each step she took. She looked a little thicker, but that was because she was constantly in the house. She didn't recognize Pop at first, but she knew his car. She couldn't get use to the fade he adorned. His thick shoulder length dreads were something that always attracted her to him, but his smooth chocolate face remained the same. As she got closer, Pop got out of the car to greet her.

"Long time no see," he said extending his arms for a hug.

"What do you want, Pop?"

"Can we go somewhere and talk?"

"Nope, I'm not into going to strange locations with niggas who aren't my boyfriend, so whatever you have to say, say it right here," Gabrielle said checking her phone. No calls from K-2. She put her phone in her purse and stared at Pop. She couldn't figure out what kept her holding onto him for so long. He was very attractive, but she didn't see what she used to see. He was a lost cause.

"Damn, like that? So I'm just some nigga now?"

"You've been that?"

"So you and that bitch nigga still together?"

"That's what you came all the way up here to ask me?"

"No," Pop said trying to mask his jealousy.

"Well, don't fucking worry about it then."

"Listen, I know that you hate me, and you have every right to, but I need you to know that I didn't not come see you cause I don't care about you."

"Why didn't you then?" Gabrielle asked letting her curiosity get the best of her again.

"I didn't come see you because my cousin got blasted then you got shot. It was hot as fuck, and I knew that if I came up to the hospital, the police would be all over a nigga."

"That's a weak-ass excuse, Pop."

"I'm being forreal, blood. I was just trying to avoid the bullshit."

"Well, it's over now. I'm fine. Was that it?"

"Have you talked to Jewel?"

"No, and I don't plan to either."

"Why not?" Pop asked disappointed. Gabrielle was his only link to Jewel.

"Cause my dad said to stay away from him. He's the one that got us into this shit."

"Got us into what? Your brother is locked up right now, and ya'll leave him for dead, but you call yourself being mad cause you think I did the same shit to you?"

"Call it what you want. I went almost eighteen years without knowing the nigga, but the minute he comes along, I almost lose my life. I just think it's better if we keep things how they are," she repeated what Joe had tried to convince her and himself, "And how you know he's in jail?"

"Everybody knows. When a nigga like Jewel goes down, the streets always know. They tryna wash him."

"So, what you want me to do?"

"Shit, I thought that being family, ya'll would have that nigga out by now. Ain't your dad a lawyer?"

"And? It's not my dad's job to get every thug nigga out of jail. What you worried about Jewel for anyway? The last time I checked you fucked with GMB."

"I know that shit is not good between us right now, but despite what happened, he's like my family or at least he was."

"Well, once again, you've wasted my time. I've put you and Jewel's bullshit behind me. I'm happy, so don't try to mess that up. You have no loyalty, and that's why you're standing here talking to me. I may not know much about this street shit, but I do know that clique hopping will get your ass killed. Straight up. I don't know why I'm still standing all in the open with you anyway. If that was all, I gotta go."

Pop knew that he had crossed those closest to him, and he didn't understand why. He had gotten too comfortable being Jewel's right hand that he didn't know how to handle the jealousy and unappreciation he felt when K-2 came along, but he knew deep down that the M.A.C. Boys was an organization that could only thrive when they put the work in. Brandon slowly but surely isolated himself in the end, and Pop didn't want the same thing to happen to him. He wanted to make amends with Gabrielle and Jewel, but his apologies were a little too late, so he couldn't say anything else as she turned around and walked away.

Gabrielle hurried to get back to her class. She left early because deep down she felt like Pop was going to profess his undying love for her. He was her first love, but he took her for granted and didn't appreciate the love she wanted to give him no matter how young and immature it was. In her feelings, she called K-2 hoping to be reassured.

"What's up, baby?" he asked answering on the first ring.

"I changed my mind. I'm not gonna kick it with Maleya. Come and get me. I just want to go home, cuddle, smoke a blunt, and watch Netflix."

"You should have called me earlier. I'm in the Bay."

"What you doing out there?"

"I came to fuck with Sacario. You said that you needed space, so I'm giving you space, boo."

"I guess."

"What you mean?"

"I mean that I think it's stupid that you took your ass all the way to Richmond to go kick it with Sacario. Why he couldn't come out here?"

"Don't be like that. I'm with you twenty-four seven. If I'm not at work, I'm with you, and if I'm not with you, I'm at work. At first a nigga was not about this space shit, but then I started thinking."

"About what?"

"Us."

Gabrielle got quiet in fear of what K-2 was going to say next. She didn't want to lose him.

"Don't get me wrong, I love you, but I can't keep pretending anymore. I'm not the nigga you want me to be. I can keep throwing these corny-ass button-ups on everyday going to the office to work for your dad for the rest of my life, or I can do what I'm really good at."

"And that is?"

"Selling dope, counting money, riding on niggas, banging for the clique. All that. I know I should want something different, but I don't.

Counterfeit *Dreams 3*

I can't keep lying to myself. Being a part of the M.A.C. Boys is all I ever wanted and now's my chance."

"You can't keep selling drugs for the rest of your life, Keith. You act like you can put that shit on a resume. I thought you put all that shit behind you?"

"I thought I did too, but Jewel has been locked up for six months, and mufuckas have lost their minds. My brothers need me, so until he gets out, I'ma be out here. It's funk season, and I need to be on the frontline period. I just can't forget where I came from. I don't want to lose you, but all this high-power faking has gotta stop. I'm not cut out for your life, Gabby. I'm cut out for this one."

"What do you want me to tell my dad? That you just quit?"

"Tell him what you want. I'm not ashamed of what I do. He lives his life one way, and I just happen to live mine another. The nigga really ain't got no choice but to respect it. I'm not his son."

"Well, he thinks you are."

"Tell him he gotta son."

Gabrielle was frustrated with K-2's fascination with the streets. She thought after she got out of the hospital that they would be able to change their lives for the better together, but he only went along with everything because he felt obligated. His guilt made him become a person he didn't even recognize.

"So when are you coming back?"

"Shit, I don't even know. It's a lot going on right now, but I'ma keep you posted, lil mama. Like I said it's 'Free Jewel' until my nigga touches down, and from the way they got him hemmed up that could be a while. I'm bout to get off here. I'll hit you later tonight though."

"I love you."

"I love you too, and stop worrying about me. I've been thugging my whole life. I'm good. These niggas know about me."

"Please just be careful."

"I am, babe. Promise. I'll talk to you later."

Gabrielle hung up the phone with disappointment covering her face. She had gotten so complacent in their relationship that she would do anything to keep K-2 around. Anything, so she dialed the only other person she could depend on.

$$$$

Sasha Ravae

Reagan walked around the house cleaning up the mess Jailen always conveniently left behind. Even though she felt as big as a house, she was determined to keep some sort of normalcy in their life. With Jewel being gone, Jailen only had her and his grandmother Paula to depend on.

"Jailen, you got your stuff? Paula will be here any minute," she yelled up the stairs. She started sleeping in the guest bedroom downstairs because walking up and down the stairs everyday was becoming harder and harder.

"Almost," he yelled back.

Reagan went into the kitchen continuing to idly clean up. When Jailen wasn't around, she had nothing to do which was the time she used to re-evaluate her life. The daily calls from Jewel were beginning to not be enough. She missed his presence, his scent. She was going crazy. Before she knew it, the doorbell rang. It was Paula. Reagan waddled to the door to open it.

"Girl, you getting huge," Paula said walking inside. She and Reagan had become somewhat close over the time Jewel had been in jail. Paula tried her hardest not to like her, but she couldn't do anything but respect her. Reagan took care of Jailen even though he wasn't hers without any problems, and not once did she complain. Paula prayed each and every night that Diamond would be the mom she used to be, but that was wishful thinking.

"Who you telling?" Reagan said closing the door.

"When are you due?"

"I'm thirty-four weeks now, so not that much longer."

"Well, you need to stay off your feet. What the doctor tell you? You don't want to mess around and be readmitted."

"I know. I'm just ready for all this to be over."

"Well, why don't you have Jewel do some of the house work? Speaking of that boy, where is he? I feel like I haven't seen him in forever."

"He's been so busy at work lately. It just seems like he's gone more than he's here. You just missed him too," Reagan lied, "He left like maybe ten, fifteen minutes before you got here." she continued to lie for Jewel in fear that Paula would take Jailen from them and there would be nothing that she could do.

Counterfeit *Dreams 3*

"Tell him when he gets home to call me in the morning. I have a few things I need to talk to him about."

"No problem, Paula." Reagan would three-way call her on the house phone just to make it look like Jewel had been home. She never said anything. She just listened. Paula mentioned to Jewel that Diamond had been coming around more and more in hopes to see Jailen. This made Paula nervous because she feared that Diamond would just up and leave with Jailen. On the outside, it looked like she was clean because Marcus' money could afford her ever increasing habit. She was always dressed in designer clothes and shoes, but Paula could still tell when she was high, so she didn't buy into her sob story. After Jewel was arrested, Diamond went into treatment. She felt like she had let things get out of control, and she wanted to make them right again, but Marcus convinced her that he loved her, and she was weak. She wanted to believe that things could be different between them, so she checked out of the program and went home with him after only a few weeks. Paula was so excited when Diamond went to treatment, so it broke her heart to find out that she left again. She didn't even recognize her own daughter anymore. Paula believed that if Jailen was really a priority for her then she would leave Marcus alone for good and go to rehab and finish, but leaving him meant leaving the drugs, and Diamond wasn't ready to let go. Paula wanted Jewel to go and fix everything, but she tried to understand that his heart was now somewhere else.

"Jailen, you ready? Your grandma is here."

Within no time, he ran down the stairs with his backpack on and one of Jewel's old hats. "Hey, Grandma," he said giving Paula a kiss.

"You got everything?"

"Yep. Bye, Reagan."

"Bye, J. I'll see you Sunday, right?"

"Right."

"Okay, have fun."

"Don't forget to have Jewel call me. It's very important."

"I won't, Paula."

$$$$$

Sasha Ravae

Gabrielle sat on the school's steps as she waited for her ride. She was disappointed in K-2's decision to return to hustling, but she was hopeful that she would be able to get him to change if all he wanted was for Jewel to get out of jail. She would do whatever it took to make that happen. As she sat deep in thought, a burgundy-colored Benz pulled up in front of her. She grabbed her purse and headed toward the car.

"Hey, baby, you been out here long? You should've called me earlier. I would've came and got you when I got off work."

"I was gonna call Dad, but I changed my mind."

"Why?" Gabrielle's mom Isabella asked.

"Keith was supposed to take me home, but I told him I was busy, so he left and went to Richmond. Long story, but I just didn't want Dad asking me hella questions." Gabrielle and her mom were very close. She talked to her about things she would never let her father know about. Isabella was very much aware of Pop and his relationship with Gabrielle as well as her relationship with K-2. She didn't approve, but she always wanted her daughters to feel like they could talk to her about anything.

"I see," she said not concerned with K-2's whereabouts. She hated her daughter's fascination with thugs. Although they were close, Isabella tried to preserve the image of her little girl. She wasn't ready for her to grow up.

"Mom, can I ask you something?" Gabrielle asked changing the subject.

"Of course."

"Do you know Jewel?"

Isabella paused as she thought of the right words to say. "Yes" was all she could come up with.

"And?" Gabrielle asked hoping to get the truth out of her mother. She knew that personal situations made her uncomfortable, but she needed to know the truth.

"Jewel is your father's first child from his previous marriage." Isabella thought about Jewel every day. Even though she loved Joe and the family they were able to create together, she couldn't help but to feel guilty. She never wanted to take him away from his son. "I met Jewel when he was maybe 8. Joe would bring him to the office from time to time to keep up with the image of being a family man, but I never interacted with him too much."

"Why not?" Gabrielle questioned. She was well aware of her mother and father's rocky start, but she wanted to hear it from Isabella's mouth. She could tell that her mother was uncomfortable as she continued to squeeze the steering wheel as she spoke, but she had nowhere to run. She had to finally face her demons as she continued to drive.

"When I met your father, he was married to Jewel's mother Laura. I respected that, and nothing ever happened between me and your father at first. We kept it completely professional, but we both couldn't deny that there was something between us. Joe wasn't happy in his marriage, and I was coming out of a relationship with Raquel's father. It was just really bad timing, but the more Joe and I worked together, the more my feelings for him grew, so I supported his decision to get a divorce because I was tired of being the other woman. I'm not proud of how we started, but your father was miserable, and I think that if it weren't for Jewel, he would have gotten a divorce long before I came along."

"So after you and Dad decided to be together, he just up and left Jewel?"

"No, that couldn't be further from the truth. Laura was bitter about me being in the picture. Joe had affairs in the past, but nothing that would jeopardize their seemingly perfect marriage, so during the divorce, Laura did her best to villainize Joe. He wasn't the father that he is today. He had to grow up a lot, but he never stopped loving his son, not for one second. He just didn't want to deal with the drama that Laura brought, so unfortunately, he was ordered to pay Jewel's mother a huge sum of money each month for child support, and she retained full physical custody of him. Your father did his best to maintain a relationship with Jewel, but Laura made it impossible, so he did what he thought was right at the time."

"Which was what?"

"He let Jewel know that he would always be there to take care of him financially, but he was tired of Laura using him as a pawn to get back at Joe. I know that he did what he did out of frustration, and it's something that kills him every day. Jewel is his only son, and he didn't fight for him. He knows now that he should have fought harder."

"Do you think that if Jewel was in trouble, Dad would help?"

"Despite what your father might say, there is nothing in this world that he wants more than to reconnect with Jewel, but he feels like it's too late. Is everything okay?"

"Well, my friend told me that Jewel is in jail. I didn't believe him, but then I looked his name up on Sac Sheriff and saw his charges. It looks like he was arrested for assault and battery and trespassing, but he hasn't been charged with anything yet, and no bail is set. As far as I know, Jewel should be able to afford a good attorney, but the lawyer he has now isn't doing his job. Do you think Daddy would look into it?"

"Jewel is an adult now, so I'm not sure of your father wants to involve himself in his affairs, or even if Jewel wants Joe involved."

"But what if Daddy could help him? I'm not saying that we'll become one big happy family or anything, but it's a start, right?"

"Gabby, that's between your father and Jewel. My concern is keeping you and Raquel safe. Period."

"Mom, I don't know any other man as my father. Daddy has been nothing but good to me these past eighteen years. To Raquel too, and she's not even his. I know that no matter how bad I mess up, he'll always be there to help me pick up the pieces. Doesn't Jewel deserve the same thing? How would you feel going through the world not having anyone to turn to? Daddy made some mistakes. Maybe this can be his chance to make things right."

Isabella knew that Jewel was in the game, and she wanted to keep that life far away from her family, but no matter what, he was still Joe's son.

"I'll talk to him, okay? Maybe he knows somebody that can help, but I doubt he'll do anything himself being that it's a conflict of interest."

"Whatever he can do is better than nothing," Gabrielle said hoping that Joe would be able to pull a few strings to get Jewel released. As much as she wanted to get to know him, she wanted K-2 to remain safe even more. She needed K-2 to let go of his hood dreams.

$$$$$

Counterfeit *Dreams 3*

K-2 posted on the porch and watched the activity in the neighborhood. The sun was shining brightly in Richmond. Neighborhood kids ran wildly through the streets taunting the small Mexican man who sold corn and spicy mangos from a cart on the corner. He missed home. Sacario came out of the trap house with a bottle of Remy in one hand and some swishers in the other. After the police raided his house, he was arrested even though they didn't find anything. He could remember the look on his wife's face as the police ransacked their house with total disregard. They took him to Sacramento because he was on Roberts' list. Sacario had been gang affiliated, so he was already in the system. He had a record, but still there was nothing to hold him on. With no witnesses or evidence, Roberts was forced to release Sacario too. Everything was hearsay, but the desperate detective was determined to stick them with anything he could. After he was released, he went home to make sure that his family was safe. He knew that they all had targets on their backs, but he stayed ready. Sacario was the only one who Jewel kept in contact with. He called Reagan almost every day to check on things. With Jewel being locked up, Golden dead, Pop M.I.A., and GMB on the rise, the M.A.C. Boys were almost nonexistent, but Sacario believed in the cause, so he never gave up on his team. When he got back to the Bay, he knew that he had to play his part. He was the last one standing until K-2 came back home.

"So how long you staying out here?"

"Damn, you tryna get rid of me already, nigga?" K-2 asked taking the green glass bottle out of Sacario's hands.

"Naw, I'm just asking. I didn't know if you were playing fresh prince of Sac or what."

"Whatever, breh, call it what you want, but a nigga's still eating though. I was getting like $55 an hour just to push a couple papers here and there. I think I was only there for show cause I swear they ain't have a nigga do shit all day."

"How you sound, blood?"

"What you mean? It was cool."

"You talking about $8,000-$9,000 a month? Nigga I see that every day. Tax free though, but shit, don't mind me. I'm not tryna knock your hustle, feel me?"

"What else you doing? And just so niggas don't get it twisted, I've hung up my tie for good."

"What? No more Starbucks with daddy dearest?"

"Fuck you, blood. Act like you remember. I'm a reptable out here in these streets, nigga," K-2 said getting angry. He had been gone for a few months, but in his heart, he still bled the streets.

"I'm just saying, I thought you was getting soft. That's all."

"Ain't shit soft over here, boy," K-2 said holding up his diamond chain against his hand, "I get money just like you do."

"Okay, blood," Sacario said holding his hands up, "So what you doing out here though, tough guy?"

"I'm back. With Jewel being locked up, I don't think that you should be out here holding it down by yourself. Shit might get ugly."

"Shit, it's been ugly. GMB is all over Sac now. They got us looking like we hiding and shit, but them niggas know not to bring that shit out here. My niggas still go hard. Believe that." Sacario looked up to Golden so much that he never wanted to fuck with anybody but the M.A.C. Boys, but he could never get used to Sacramento enough to move there, so he started slanging out in the Bay. His squad grew and grew, but Golden always kept an eye on things. But with him gone, the city was no longer fair game. GMB was killing niggas left and right just to continue to make a name for themselves. It seemed like every week the M.A.C. Boys continued to fall back. They had no support or direction. Things just weren't the same.

"So what's the plan? I've been itching to blast a few niggas."

"I'm just waiting on word from Jewel."

Chapter 2

Jewel sat in his cell and stared at the wall. He couldn't believe he was still in County. Every time he went to court, the date was rescheduled. The M.A.C. Boys had several lawyers on retainer who made sure that not one of them would have to see the inside of a jail cell, but this time, it was different. His lawyer Peter Alvarez was dumbfounded at the way they were treating Jewel. He was doing everything in his power to get him out, but nothing worked. Alvarez petitioned the court to ask that Jewel be released on bail, but the judge denied that motion too. He had it in for Jewel.

"Sanchez, get up," a small, white guard yelled through the metal bars, "You have a visitor."

Even though he was still in Sac, he didn't want anybody to come and see him. He didn't want to further implicate himself.

"Who is it?"

The guard remained silent. Jewel stood up and waited for the cell door to open. The sound of metal sliding against metal made him sick to his stomach. Being locked up was for other niggas. He was insulted that he was even there. After the door was open, the guard came and handcuffed him for safety precautions. Jewel followed alongside him as he was led across the tier. Instead of going to the regular visiting area, the guard led him to a small conference room. Jewel was confused because he had never been in the unfamiliar area. The guard knocked on the door and waited for a response.

"Come in," Jewel heard a man's voice from the other side of the door say. When the guard opened the door, Jewel saw his father Joe sitting down at the table dressed to kill. He oozed money.

"What is this?" Jewel asked confused.

"Hey, son," Joe said hurt to see him locked up like an animal. He had seen many people go to jail, but he never imagined when Jewel was growing up that he would too. "Derrick, can you give us a moment please?"

"No problem, Mr. Sanchez." Joe was well known for what he did. As a defense attorney, he had encountered many people, so his connections were invaluable.

Joe waited until the guard was out of the room before he spoke, "How you feeling?"

Jewel continued to stand up uncomfortable with their interaction. He had never really been alone with Joe, so it was like looking into the face of a familiar stranger.

"I've been better," he said scratching his head.

"So what happened?"

"They got me on some bullshit charge. I'm paying my lawyer $150,000 to still be sitting in this mothafucka."

"I want to help," Joe said staring Jewel in the eyes.

"Why?"

"Because you're my son, Jewel."

"And? That ain't ever meant shit before. I don't need your help. I'ma figure this shit out on my own."

"Jewel, the Moore's are very influential in this city, so if Marcus Moore said you were trespassing and that you assaulted him, the judge is going to believe him. Marcus' father is a very generous donor to the Department of Justice."

"How do you know about Marcus?"

"I checked on your case before I came here. I think I can get you out with maybe probation and some anger management classes. I just need you to be honest with me."

"Like I said I don't want your help."

"So you're willing to stay locked up in here instead of letting me help?"

"Shit, if I have to. Listen, Joe, I appreciate the offer, but I've made it on my own this long. What makes you think that I need you now?"

"I know that I have made some mistakes in the past, but I know that God brought you back into my life for a reason. Jewel, you are my only son, my first born. There wasn't a day that went by that I didn't think of you. I wanted to be there, but your mother made it impossible. She couldn't accept that I wanted to end our marriage and that I was happy with someone else. Genuinely happy. I left her, Jewel, but I didn't want to leave you too."

"Man, fuck all that. You made your choice back then, so it is what it is," he said not wanting to relive his childhood. He knew that there was nothing that could keep him away from his son, so Joe had no excuse. His mother Laura never paid any attention to him unless there were other people around. She would make it a point to seem like she had the perfect marriage and family, but in reality, her first and only love was alcohol. Joe and Laura got married more out of a business arrangement orchestrated by their families. Laura was told that she would eventually fall in love with Joe, but as the years passed, she just fell in love with the lifestyle that their marriage provided. Growing up, Jewel looked up to his father. He tried his best to get Joe to notice him because he admired everything about him, but Joe's career was his only concern at that time, so Jewel spent most of his time alone. He didn't really have too many friends, so when he found Brandon and Golden, he gravitated to them immediately because he craved that family-like bond, and they gave that to him. All his niggas in the M.A.C. Boys were like brothers to Jewel, and he pledged his loyalty to each and every one of them. He would put his life on the line for them. He bled in the streets for them. Joe leaving Jewel to start another family with Isabella changed who he was, and now he couldn't remember the young boy he used to be.

"Jewel, I've changed. I just need you to give me a chance to show you that. I know that I can never make up for the time that I've missed, but let me try to use the time we have now."

Jewel felt trapped. He had bottled up his emotions towards Joe, and he did his best to tuck them away, but sitting right in front of his father made him feel like the lost little boy he left behind all over again.

"How'd you know I was in here?"

Joe thought about it before he spoke, "Gabrielle brought it to my attention."

"So for over ten years you haven't bothered to seek me out, but your daughter tells you I'm in jail, and you book it down here? For what though?"

"Your sister almost died. My mind has been wrapped up in keeping her safe. I'm sorry."

"Keep her safe from niggas like me, right?"

"I didn't say that."

"You didn't have to. You said everything you had to say at the hospital. Listen, Joe, I appreciate the offer, but I'm my own man, and I'll figure this shit out. If I have to hire Johnny Cochran's ghost, I'ma get out of here. Go be with your family," Jewel said getting up out of his seat. He couldn't believe that Joe was any different. His heart was too hard to think otherwise. He knocked on the door signaling the guard outside.

"All set?"

"Yeah."

Joe sat at the table unable to say anything. He didn't know how to get through to Jewel. He knew he had mess up, but he just hoped that he hadn't lost his son forever.

Jewel walked back to his cell irritated by his father's seemingly ingenuine attempt to help him. For over a decade, he had made it on his own without any help or guidance from Joe, and he didn't want to start now. He grabbed his phone from underneath his bunk, and decided to call the only person who could ease my mind.

"Hello?" Reagan asked answering on the first ring.

"You sleep?"

"No, this little boy has been kicking me all night. I swear I can't wait til this shit is over with."

"Is Jailen at Paula's?" Jewel asked changing the subject. As much as he loved Reagan and wanted to support her, he didn't want the constant reminder that she was actually pregnant with Brandon's baby.

"Yeah, she came and got him last night. She wanted me to tell you to call her."

"For what?"

"I don't know. She just said that she needed to talk to you and it's important."

"Call her on three-way for me."

"What's the number?" Reagan asked with an attitude. As much as she held Jewel down, she missed him, and she wanted to talk to him, but he was always concerned with everything and everybody else.

"488-9864."

"Hold on," she said clicking over.

"Jewel?"

"Hey, Paula, what's up?"

"You at home?"

"Yeah, I just got back a couple of hours ago. What's up? How's Jailen?"

"Everything is good. He's in here eating up all my food."

"You know that boy can eat," Jewel said missing his son.

Counterfeit *Dreams 3*

"Who you telling? Anyway, I needed to talk to you because I don't think that it's a good idea that he comes over here for the weekends anymore."

"What you mean?" Jewel questioned. He was confused because he knew how close they were to each other. Paula lived for her grandson.

"Diamond has been popping up lately. Luckily, it's been on the week days, but still. I'm just afraid that if he's here that she'll just take him and leave, and in her state, that's the last thing my baby needs. She keeps saying that she's gonna check herself into a treatment program, but each time, she either leaves the program early or she doesn't go at all. I just don't think it's safe for him to be here right now."

"I understand," Jewel said appreciating that she was always looking out for Jailen. He couldn't even believe what Diamond was going through. In high school, she barely even drank. He didn't know what hold Marcus had over her, but his son's safety came before her desire to still pretend to be a mom.

"I know that it's gonna be hard for him to understand all of this right away, but I just think that it's for the best."

"I'll have a talk with him. Don't worry about it. Maybe a trip somewhere will take his mind off things for a while."

"That would be good for him, Jewel, and I know that between you and that girl, he's in good hands. He's very fond of her, you know? As much as it hurts me to know that Diamond isn't there for him like she should be, I am very thankful that Reagan has been able to pick up the slack. Pregnancy and all," Paula laughed.

Jewel was happy that Reagan was holding it down. He knew how she felt in the beginning when she first found out about him having a kid with Diamond, but just as he had to accept her child with Brandon, he was glad to know that she had done the same thing with Jailen.

"I'ma keep him for the rest of the week since he doesn't have school, but I'll bring him back next Sunday."

"No, problem, Paula. You guys have fun."

"You wanna talk to him?"

"Yeah, let me holla at him real quick."

"Hold on," she said putting the phone down, "Jailen come here for a second. Your dad is on the phone."

Sasha Ravae

A few moments later, Jailen hopped on the phone with excitement in his voice, "Hey, Dad."

"What's up, son? What you doing?"

"Nothing, just eating and watching TV. How's work?"

"It's work. I'd rather be home with you guys."

"Do you know when you're coming home yet?"

"Not yet, but I'm hoping soon. I just have a few more loose ends to tie up, but after that I'm coming straight home. How are things going with you?"

"They're okay."

"That's good, J. Well, I don't want to keep you. I know it's your weekend with your grandma, so I'll let you guys get back to it, okay? I'll call you Sunday when you get home."

"Okay, Dad. Love you."

"Love you too."

"Bye." Jailen quickly handed the phone back to Paula as he returned to his favorite show *SpongeBob*.

"Okay, Jewel, I'll see you Sunday, right?"

"I'm leaving out again tonight for work, so I might not be back in town by then."

"Jewel, it seems like I haven't seen you in months. Whatever little project you've been working on can wait. Your son needs you right now. I'll see you next Sunday," Paula said hanging up.

Jewel didn't want her to know that he was in jail because he didn't want her to think that Jailen had two irresponsible parents. In fear of his child's wellbeing, he began to panic.

"Fuck, I gotta get out of here," he yelled.

"Have you heard anything from your lawyer?" Reagan asked after making sure she had clicked over and Paula was no longer on the line.

"Yeah, but he keeps saying the same shit. I'm bout to fire that nigga forreal. It don't make no sense with the amount of money I'm paying him, but for the first time ever in my life, it seems like my money can't help me."

Jewel had done everything in his power to get out of jail. Money was no object for him. He had more than enough to hire the best lawyers, but it didn't matter. Marcus' father had more influence, and Marcus had a point to prove. He wanted Jewel to know that Diamond was his and his alone.

"Something's gotta give though."

"Have you talked to your dad?"

"Why you ask that? Jewel asked defensively.

"I mean I know he doesn't do defense law anymore, but he has to know a few people who can help, right?"

"You sound just like that nigga."

"What? You talked to him?" Reagan asked excitedly.

"He showed up talking about he wanted to help out or whatever."

"Jewel, that's great," she squealed.

"I told him I didn't need his help."

"Jewel…"

"No, fuck that. Don't 'Jewel' me. I don't need him for shit. He thinks that if he gets me out then that's gonna erase all the bullshit he put my family through, but it won't. I'd rather be up in this mothafucka then to give him the satisfaction."

"What about your own family? What about Jailen, me, and the baby? This has nothing to do with Joe. If he can help put all of this behind you, why would you not let him help?"

"Like I said I don't need it," Jewel snapped, "Now drop it. I'ma figure this out on my own. I promise you that, but let me get off of here. I'll try to call you tomorrow."

"I love you," Reagan said disappointed with his stubbornness.

"I love you too."

$$$$$

A Week Later…

"Your Honor, there's no need for my client to continue to be held in custody. Even with the warrant, the D.A. didn't find anything that connects Mr. Sanchez to these alleged crimes. It's all hearsay," said Jewel's newly acquired lawyer.

"Mr. King, would you like to respond?" the judge asked impatient with the prosecution. It had been over six months since Jewel had been taking into custody, and they failed to provide a concrete case against him.

"We have reason to believe that Mr. Sanchez is the head of the M.A.C. Boys, an unlawful and dangerous organization in the

community, Your Honor. Detective Roberts was able to obtain
testimony from people who can connect Mr. Sanchez to several
murders."

"But none are willing to testify?"

"No, not at this time, Your Honor."

"I request that a writ of habeas corpus be issued because this is
insane. There are no bodies linked to him, no illegal money, nothing.
My client is a single father just trying to get back home to his son. He
felt like the mother of his child was in danger. She called him from
Mr. Moore's home for god's sake. Mr. Sanchez did what I think any of
us would do. He is being held unlawfully, and I request that he be
released."

"Mr. King, you have twenty-four hours to decide if any charges are
going to be filed. If there is nothing further, Mr. Sanchez, you are free
to go."

Jewel turned around and assumed the position as the bailiff came
and released the tight, cold, metal handcuffs which bounded his wrists.
He was instructed to follow the bailiff and go to retrieve his
belongings, but he never took his eyes from his lawyer. He didn't
know where he came from, but Jewel was thankful nonetheless. After
signing a few papers and receiving his personal property, he was
released back out into the free world. As the gate opened, he was face-
to-face with his father Joe.

"I told you I'd get you out."

"Thanks," Jewel said wanting to keep the conversation short.

"Do you wanna talk about what happened?"

"Joe, I already told you what I know. Some dirty-ass cop is trying
to pin some shit on me that has nothing to do with me. Why? I don't
fucking no. I apologize that Gabrielle got hurt, but this is my life and
now you know, so just stay away from me, okay? It'll be better for
everybody." Jewel walked out of the jail leaving his father behind.

$$$$$

Reagan waddled around the house preparing for Jailen to come
home. Being a prisoner in her own home gave her a lot of free time, so
she used it to get the baby room together. She did a lot of on-line
shopping since she never left the house, and everyday a new package

came for either the baby or Jailen. She had gained almost fifty pounds from her pregnancy, so she refrained from indulging on herself. She felt hideous. She promised that she wouldn't buy herself anything other than the basics until she delivered and got her body back together. Her hair had grown wildly down her back, but Reagan only kept it in a messy bun having no energy to fix herself up in any kind of way. With Jewel being gone, she really didn't see the need in it. She was excited to meet her son, but she was more excited to get back to the person she used to be. She barely recognized herself anymore. These were the moments that made her think of Robyn. She didn't have anyone to talk to, and it was driving her crazy. She missed her friend.

Reagan went into the kitchen and began to make dinner for Jailen's return. She made baked chicken, rice-a-roni, and canned green beans. The simpler the better; she was still learning. Just as she was about to put the chicken in the oven, the doorbell rang. Reagan knew that it was too early to be Jailen, so she assumed that another one of her purchases had arrived. She slowly walked to the door making sure to check the peephole before she opened it. Seeing who it was, she immediately snatched the door open.

"Pop?"

"Hey, Reagan, it's been a minute," he said staring down at her belly. The last time he had seen her, she wasn't even showing yet.

"Oh my god, how have you been?" she asked grabbing him for a hug, but her belly got in the way.

"I've been straight. Can we talk?"

"Yeah, yeah, of course, come in." Reagan stared at Pop's face noticing how much he had matured. He looked so much older. "Is everything okay? You know Jewel's not here, right?" She closed the door behind them and led Pop into the living room. Even though he hadn't been around in a while, she just assumed that he had heard about Jewel being in jail.

"Actually, I just needed to talk to you. You're the only one I can talk to."

"What's going on?" Reagan asked becoming nervous. She knew that Jewel and Pop weren't on the best of terms, but she didn't know exactly why.

"How's Jewel holding up?"

"He's okay I guess. He's trying to hang in there, but this shit with this case is fucking with him."

"They not tryna let him out?"

"It doesn't seem like it."

"I wish I was able to talk to the nigga face-to-face, but you're the closest person to him, so I just need you to relay a message to him for me."

"He should be calling pretty soon. You should talk to him. I know it would be good for him to hear your voice."

"Naw, this is some shit that I need to tell him in person."

"Okay," Reagan said scared about what Pop was going to say. She knew that Jewel looked out for him and had always looked at him like a little brother, but over the time he had been locked up, Jewel never mentioned Pop once.

"I don't know if Jewel told you or not, but Golden is dead." Reagan remained silent. "I was with the niggas who shot Golden and Will. I left the M.A.C. Boys out of anger, but I never intended for anybody to get hurt. I was just tryna make money. Jewel dropped me because he didn't want something to happen to me. I know that now, but it's too late. I don't expect him to forgive me because I betrayed him and all of M.A.C. I'm done banging. I don't have it in me no more, but I couldn't live with myself if anything happened to Jewel."

"What are you talking about, Pop?"

"This nigga Kisino used to be partners with Golden until he got greedy. When Golden announced that he was stepping down and passing everything to Jewel, he flipped and from that point on, he had it in for Golden and Jewel. Kisino feels like the empire that Golden built belongs to him."

"What does Golden's beef with some nigga have to do with Jewel?" As much as Reagan loved him, she hated the life he chose to live. Everything he did made her scared that she was going to lose him.

"Jewel wouldn't budge. Kisino thought that he could strong arm Jewel because Brandon had been letting Kisino know Jewel and Golden's every move. After Golden passed the torch to Jewel, it had Brandon feeling some kind of way too. Kisino helped to breed the hate that Brandon developed for Jewel. He used his jealousy for his own benefit."

Counterfeit *Dreams 3*

Hearing Brandon's name made Reagan cringe. "How do you know all this?"

"My cousin fucked with Kisino and his clique GMB tough. That's how I got introduced to him. Kisino felt like if Golden wasn't going to hand over the M.A.C. Boys then he was gonna take it, so he had Will killed, and he killed Golden right in front of Jewel and Sacario. It was a message to Jewel. I never meant for any of this to happen. I didn't know it was gonna go this far. Now three people are dead, and I feel like I'm partly responsible."

"Three?"

"My cousin KP was killed by Sacario's brother. I tried to stop it, but I couldn't. That's how it goes out here though. If you kill a nigga, you have to prepare yourself for the blow back. My cousin knew what was up. I mean as fucked up as it is, I'm just glad Gabrielle didn't get hurt that bad. She doesn't have anything to do with this shit."

"Who's Gabrielle?"

"Jewel's sister," Pop said presuming Reagan already knew about his newfound family.

"Sister?" She tried to keep up with Pop's story, but it was hard to because Jewel didn't let her into that part of his life. He felt like the less she knew the better for her own safety. "Jewel's an only child."

"Not on his dad's side," Pop said plainly, "Listen, I know that this is a lot to take in, but I just wanted to come here to warn Jewel. Kisino made it clear that he's not gonna stop until niggas either get down with GMB or until there's not one M.A.C. Boy left standing."

Reagan and Pop talked for the next two hours about everything that happened over the past few months. She had a lot of questions because she needed to understand the life which Jewel refused to let her into. Pop told her everything from beginning to end hoping that she would see how sorry he was. He never meant for anyone to lose their lives let alone his own family member. He owed everything to Jewel and Golden. He didn't know where he would be if it wasn't for them. He knew that there was nothing that he could say to make things right again, but he had to try.

"I hit up Jewel's sister Gabrielle about talking to their dad. I mean I thought that since he's a lawyer that maybe he could help Jewel, but after everything that happened, she wasn't fucking with me."

"I talked to Jewel's dad, and I got the same response from him too, but then Jewel said he came up there and told him that he wanted to help, but he said he didn't need it."

"Jewel's smart. He knows what he's doing, but honestly, it's good that he's in there. It's safer than being out here."

"I guess," Reagan said unsure of what to do to help Jewel. She knew that he was a drug dealer, but she didn't know how deep he was in the game. "So what now?"

Before Pop could answer, the doorbell rang.

"Stay here. I'll be right back," she said closing the double doors that led to the living room. She looked up at the clock and knew that it was Paula and Jailen. Paula tried to have him home around the same time, so that he could eat dinner and have enough time to get ready for school the next day. Reagan opened the door hoping to have Paula in and out, so that she and Pop could finish their conversation. As soon as she opened the door, Jailen shot inside expecting to see Jewel.

"Is Dad here yet? Grandma said he was coming home today," he said barely able to speak.

"Ummmm..." Reagan was mad that Paula had set Jailen's hopes up so high. "Why don't you go put your stuff in your room and get ready for dinner, okay? And we'll talk about it when you come back downstairs."

"Okay." He ran up the stairs with his bags in hand excited at the possibility of finally seeing Jewel.

Reagan waited until he was upstairs before she spoke, "Paula, why would you tell Jailen that Jewel was coming home today?" She was irritated that she was going to have to be the one to disappoint him.

"Because the last time I talked to Jewel, I told him that he needed to make his son a priority. With everything going on with Diamond, I thought that he would understand that."

"He does, but with work and everything, he's been very busy."

"You know what? Jewel hasn't been here for what seems like months. Every time I drop off or pick Jailen up, it's just you here. No offense, but nobody is that damn busy. Let me find out something else is going on," Paula said becoming more and more suspicious.

"Something like what? Jewel has been out of town the past few weeks for work. That's it. That's all."

"You wouldn't lie to me now would you?"

Counterfeit *Dreams 3*

"There's no need to."

"Well, good then. Let's call him and see where he's at. He should be able to explain why he's not here to be with his son, but his pregnant girlfriend is, right?" Paula asked pulling out her cell phone.

"He may not answer. He doesn't really get service where he's at."

"It's ringing," Paula said never taking her eyes off Reagan. She didn't know what was going on, but she felt like she and Jewel were hiding something. She just didn't know what.

"Hello?" Jewel asked answering the phone before it went to voicemail.

"Jewel, where are you? I'm here to drop Jailen off, and you're not here. You said…"

"I know what I said, Paula," he said walking into the house from the garage. He set his bags down on the floor and grabbed Reagan and kissed her on the cheek. Her eyes got big and her mouth dropped at the sight of him. He looked like he had never left. He was shaven, had a fresh cut, and new clothes. Reagan was shocked. She had no idea that he was getting out.

"My flight got delayed," Jewel lied, "But I made it. Is everything okay?" He never took his hands off of the small of Reagan's back, and she couldn't take her eyes off of him.

"Well, I guess it is now," Paula said with a side-eye, but she decided to let it go, "Let me say goodbye to my baby before I get out of here. Jailen."

Yes, Grandma," he said coming to the top of the stairs.

"Come give me a kiss before I go."

Jailen walked down the stairs until he saw Jewel. He forgot about his grandmother's request and bolted toward his father. "Dad, you made it." He squeezed Jewel around his waist as hard as he could. He missed him more than he would ever know.

"I told you I was coming back, son. I got done with work sooner than I thought, so I came straight here."

"I'm so happy you're home, Dad."

"Me too, J."

"Ump humph," Paula interrupted, "Excuse me."

"Sorry, Grandma." Jailen walked over to her and kissed her on the lips.

Sasha Ravae

"Grandma has some things to do next weekend, so I'ma let you spend some time with your dad, okay?"

"Okay," Jailen said unwilling to protest.

"You gon' call me?"

"Yep."

"Okay, I'll talk to you soon, baby. Have a good night."

"Okay, love you."

"Love you too, and Jewel, thank you for keeping your promise. He really needs you right now."

"I know."

"Talk to you guys later."

Jewel walked over to the door and closed it behind Paula because Reagan was still unable to move.

"You cooking?" he asked smelling something in the air.

"Shit." Reagan ran into the kitchen to find her chicken completely burned, and the rice was still sitting on the stove uncooked. "Sorry, I forgot I was cooking," she yelled from the kitchen.

"Okay, plan B, you wanna get pizza?" Jewel offered.

"Sure, I can order it online. Reagan has me do it all the time," Jailen admitted.

"Sounds good to me. Get whatever you want."

"Okay, I'll be right back." Jailen ran back upstairs to complete the pizza order form online that he had become too familiar with.

Jewel walked into the kitchen where Reagan was trying to discard the burnt chicken legs she had been baking hours before. "I'm so sorry. I completely forgot," she said throwing away the pot of rice-a-roni that had been soaking in water.

"It's good," Jewel said staring at Reagan. She had changed so much in the six months he had been gone. "I knew it was only a matter of time before you burned down the house anyway."

"Shut up," she said throwing a dish towel at him.

"Come here."

Reagan walked over to Jewel embarrassed by how she looked. She felt huge, but if she knew he was coming home, she would have dressed up a little. He wrapped his arms tightly around her ever growing waist and penetrated her soul with his eyes. He wanted to take in every piece of her.

Counterfeit *Dreams 3*

"How are you even here right now?" She had a million questions racing through her head.

"Shhhh...." Jewel lightly pressed his lips onto hers soothing her anxiety, and Reagan melted into his arms as if nothing or no one existed around them. He was finally home, and that was all that mattered.

"What...happened?" she tried to ask between kisses.

"I'm home. Can we just leave it at that?"

"No, Jewel, we have a lot to talk about, but first, I need to tell you something."

"Well, whatever it is, it can wait. A nigga has been down for months. All I wanna do is take a fucking shower and spend the night with my family if that's okay?"

"That's fine, but I need you to know..."

"Aye, Reagan, I'ma get outta here. Thank you though," Pop said making his way out of the living room. He couldn't hear anything, so he had no idea that Jewel was even there.

"What the fuck is he doing here?" Jewel asked looking back and forth between Pop and Reagan.

"Jewel," she began.

"Uncle Pop?" Jailen screamed out in excitement. Out of all of Jewel's potnahs, he was Jailen's favorite. Pop treated him like family, but after everything that happened, he suddenly wasn't around anymore, and Jailen definitely noticed.

"What's up, man? How you been?" Pop asked giving Jailen dap.

"I'm good. You staying for dinner?" he asked hopefully, "Dad, I ordered the pizza."

"Hey, Jailen, let's go find a movie to watch while we wait for the pizza to get here, okay? You dad and Uncle Pop need to talk for a minute," Reagan said trying to diffuse the situation.

"I'll be right there, J," Jewel said never taking his eyes off Pop. "Okay, Dad."

"Jewel, please just hear him out, okay?" Reagan said scared of what he was going to do. Loyalty meant everything to him, and Pop had betrayed his trust more than once.

Jewel waited until Reagan and Jailen left the kitchen before he spoke, "Like I said what the fuck are you doing here?"

"I didn't think you would be home. You got out today?"

"Don't worry about it, nigga. Why are you in my house with my girl and my son?" Jewel was furious. He believed in Pop. He wanted more for him than the street life they both agreed to live, but he proved to be just a typical street nigga.

"I came to talk to Reagan."

"About what?"

"Look, I know that I'm the last person you wanna see, and I wouldn't be surprised if you wanted my head like the rest of these niggas, but I came to talk to Reagan cause I know that she's the only person that can get through to you. I fucked up. I know that. There's nothing that I can do or say that will change anything that happened. If I could bring Will and Golden back right now, I would."

"But you can't, so give me one reason why I shouldn't shoot you in the fucking face right now?"

"Jewel, when you told me that I was out the clique, I lost my mind. Between you and Brandon, I put in more than enough work to prove myself. I felt like I was that nigga, so when you told me that K-2 was taking my place, I didn't understand that."

"Do you think that decision was easy? I rocked with you when nobody else would. After you got shot, I honestly didn't think you was gon' make it. I asked God to spare you, and he did, so I had to keep my end of the deal, and that was to keep you alive. K-2 was never a replacement, but Sacario vouched for him. That was it. You not being in the clique anymore was for your own benefit, nigga. Shit was crazy. It still is."

"I get that now. I went to GMB cause my cousin was getting dough with Kisino. I felt like if I couldn't make money with ya'll, I might as well get it from somewhere else, but I never knew he had planned all that shit, blood. He was using me to get to you, and I let him, but I swear, I didn't know. You gotta believe me."

"I don't gotta believe shit. You watched two of your own get gunned down all for a dollar? Fuck all that."

"By the time I knew what was really going on, it was too late. After Kisino killed Golden, I dipped. I told him that he was gon' have to kill me too. I was done. The shit just got outta hand."

"Outta hand? Golden is dead. Will is dead. That's more than shit just getting outta hand, nigga."

"My cousin got killed too. K-2 shot him right in front of me."

Counterfeit *Dreams 3*

"And?" Jewel asked coldly, "Am I supposed to give a fuck?"

"No, but that's the reality of the situation. I gotta live with their deaths. If it wasn't for me, none of this would have ever happened, but it did."

"So what do you want from me?" Jewel asked unmoved by his confession.

"Your forgiveness."

"That's something I can't give you. You were like a brother to me. I mean all my niggas are like my brothers, but you and Brandon were the closest things to me. Golden gave me everything, and I wanted to do the same for you, but I knew that you were meant for more. I saw something in you even when you didn't see it in yourself. Do you really think that I would leave you for dead?"

"It's not about that. I'm a grown-ass man, and I can maintain on my own. I didn't need you giving a nigga an allowance. I know I fucked up, but I want to make things right. Kisino isn't gonna stop until you give him what he wants."

"And what's that?"

"The M.A.C. Boys. After Golden stepped down and handed you the business, Brandon was letting him know about everything that went on. Kisino knows more about the operations than a lot of these niggas. He's just waiting to strike. Does anybody know you're out?"

"Naw."

"You need to keep it like that. Just take Reagan and Jailen and get outta Sac."

"What the fuck do I look like? That's the problem now. Everybody thinks that I can't function without Golden holding my hand. It's about time I remind mufuckas why I am who I am. Ain't no bitch in me, nigga. Never has been."

"Jewel, unless you ready to go to war, you should just let this shit go."

"Naw, blood, Golden's death isn't gonna be in vain. I'ma personally make sure that Kisino and every bitch-made nigga in GMB pay for the blood they spilled, and that's on Golden."

"I know this don't mean shit, but if you need me, I'm here."

Jewel didn't know who he could trust anymore. He had been wrong so many times. The people he trusted the most seemed to be the ones who always fucked him over, but he had no other choice. Kisino was out for blood, so Jewel had to be ready. After him and Brandon fell out, the clique was divided, and he had to get everybody back on the same page. He couldn't accept being disrespected by out of town niggas in his city. Kisino had to pay for what he did to Golden and Will, and Pop was the only person who could lead Jewel right to him.

"We'll talk more later, blood. I got some shit to put in motion first, but I'ma get at you." He didn't want to reveal too much to Pop because he still didn't trust him. He had to learn the hard way that everyone had a motive, and he didn't know what Pop's was.

"Alright, blood." Pop knew that it was going to take time to get back in Jewel's good graces again, but he was willing to do whatever it took.

Jewel walked him to the door. "This doesn't mean that shit is just squashed."

"I know, but I'm willing to do whatever it takes to make this thing right again. I at least owe you that."

"Don't tell anybody you seen me, okay?"

"I got you," Pop said disappearing into the night.

"Is everything alright?" Reagan asked hearing the front door close.

"Yeah, it's good."

"I know that it's none of my business, but you should give Pop another chance."

"It doesn't work like that, Reagan, and you're right, this shit is none of your business, so please just drop it."

"Jewel, he told me everything. I know that he fucked up in the worst way possible, but everybody deserves a second chance, right?"

"I don't give second chances."

"You gave me one," she said looking him in the eye.

"That was different."

"How? Jewel, if you forgot, I'm pregnant with your dead friend's baby. I cheated on you. I hurt you more than I think I'll ever be able to understand, but you still found it in your heart to forgive me."

Reagan didn't make Jewel feel any better. She only reiterated the fact that he trusted those he shouldn't of, but no more.

"Drop it, Reagan. I know what I'm doing."

"Okay."

Ding. Dong.

"That's probably the pizza."

Counterfeit *Dreams 3*

"I got it," she said hurrying to the door. She was starving. When she opened it, she gave the pizza guy the money, and he handed her two boxes of pizza, a two-liter soda, and some hot wings. That was her and Jailen's usual.

"Thank you. Keep the change," she said closing the door. "All I'm saying is that if you could forgive me after everything I've put you through, maybe you can forgive Pop too." She walked into the kitchen placing the food down on the counter. "Jailen, the food is here," she yelled.

"You want me to make your plate?"

"Naw, I'm not hungry," Jewel said. He was tired emotionally and physically. He wasn't prepared to see Pop. It was too much for him. He was hurt more than anything else, but he would never let anyone know it. "I think I'ma lay it down. I'm hella tired."

"You need anything?"

"Naw." Jewel walked out of the kitchen giving Jailen a hug as he passed by. He knew he had a lot to deal with, but that night, he just wanted to turn his mind off.

Chapter 3

Diamond rolled over in the king-size bed wearing nothing but a thong. She leaned over the night stand and snorted a line of white powder that sat on top. She didn't know what day or time it was, or how long they had been in that hotel room. All she knew was that she and Marcus were together. After the incident with Jewel, She was determined to get clean and take her life back. She couldn't recognize herself. She had lost thirty pounds, and on her frame, the weight difference was definitely noticeable. Diamond hated how her mom looked at her. She hated not being with her son on a daily basis, so treatment seemed like the only solution, but each time she went, Marcus would find her and flash his doctor credentials, which permitted him to visit with her, and every time, he was able to convince her that she didn't need treatment and that they could stop using drugs together. Diamond needed anything to believe in because she didn't believe in herself, but once she returned to her life with Marcus, the drinking, the drugs, and the partying continued. Soon Diamond began having sex with other women just to appease him. She hated the path that her life was on, but she didn't know how to let go. She somehow began to crave the dysfunction. She was starting to forget who she was before it.

"What time is it?" Diamond asked as she let the effects of the cocaine kick in.

"11:00 p.m., why?" Marcus sat off to the side too high to move.

"I was gonna call Jailen, but never mind, he's probably already at his dad's."

"Probably not," Marcus laughed.

"Why you say that?"

"Cause Jewel's not there. My father made sure that he won't be bothering us ever again, baby."

"And how'd he manage that?" she asked sitting up. She and Jewel had no communication with each other whatsoever, but she assumed when she spoke with the police and corroborated his story that he would be released.

"Because he was trying to take you from me, Diamond, and I can't have that."

Counterfeit *Dreams 3*

"Marcus, nobody is taking me anywhere. Now where is Jewel?" she asked beginning to panic.

Marcus refused to answer. As much as she tried to reassure him that she and Jewel were over, he didn't believe her.

Diamond ran over to the other side of the room and grabbed her phone from out of her purse. She called Jewel, but there was no answer. "Marcus, I swear if anything happened to Jewel, I'm gonna…"

"You're going to what, Diamond?" he mocked. She always threatened to leave him, but she never went anywhere. He provided her entire life.

The sound of Jewel's phone going unanswered made her sick to her stomach. The only other person she could think to call was her mom Paula. She answered on the first ring.

"Diamond, do you know what time it is?"

"I'm sorry for calling so late, but is Jailen with you still?"

"No, he's with Jewel. Why do you ask?"

At that moment, Diamond felt like a weight had been lifted off of her chest. "I was just checking. Is everything okay?"

"Everything is fine, Diamond. Despite you being in and out of that little boy's life, he is still being taken care of. You made your choice loud and clear that you no longer want to be a part of that. Am I right, or am I wrong?"

"That's still my son," she snapped, "I gave birth to Jailen. Not you. I raised him by myself for nine years."

"And then you stopped."

"It's not like that."

"You let that man and those drugs come in between the only person who truly depended on you. Now you have to live with that."

"Mom, I'm trying."

"I'll believe it when I see it, Diamond. Now goodbye. I'm going to sleep." Paula refused to entertain her delusions. She wanted nothing more in the world than to get her daughter back from Marcus' grip, but she wasn't going to hold her breath in the meantime.

Diamond set her phone down on the bed in complete defeat. She and her mother had always had a rocky relationship, but ever since they had reconnected, she felt like Paula had her back until she met Marcus. In the process, she had managed to lose her son and her relationship with her mom. She didn't know if it was worth it anymore.

"I can't do this," she said with her head down.

"Do what? Jailen's fine, right?"

"My mom said he's with Jewel. Thank God."

"What? But he's supposed to be...," Marcus said to himself.

"Marcus, from the moment I met you, I've become a person that I despise. I can't even look at myself in the mirror anymore. I thought that I loved you, but now I realize that it's the drugs that I love. I don't give a fuck about you." Diamond knew that she sounded cold, but the words needed to be said. "And you don't give a fuck about me either. I'm just your black girl show piece, but I can't do this anymore. If I don't get back to how things used to be, I might lose my son forever. Even though I'm happy that Jewel is able to be there for Jailen, this shit here," she said pointing around the room, "isn't worth sacrificing my son over. I know that I've said this a million and one times before, but this time I mean it. I'm done." Diamond tried to sober herself up. Her head was in a fog, but she was determined to get as far away from Marcus as she could.

"You're right. You do always say this. If you want space that's one thing, but leaving me is far from an option."

"And why is that?" Diamond asked as she threw her clothes in her suitcase disorganized.

"Because you need me. I take care of you," he said plainly. His money always allowed him to do what he wanted, and this time would be no different.

"Not anymore." She grabbed her clothes that lie on the floor and quickly put them on. When she was done, she grabbed her bags and purse and threw on her sunglasses and headed for the door. She hated that this was her life. She and Marcus were always fighting, and she was always leaving storming out of hotel rooms. She had to make this her last time. Marcus disregarded everything that Diamond said. The drugs usually made her emotional, so he never took her seriously. Before she reached the door, he shot up and ran to her snatching the bags out of her hand and blocking the door.

"I love you."

"Marcus, please move. I'm tired of my life being like this. Just let me go. Please."

Counterfeit *Dreams 3*

"You're tired of your life being like what?" he asked as he slid his hand across her face. She quickly turned her head.

"What do you mean like what? Like this," Diamond yelled, "You treat me like your live-in prostitute. I had a family before this. I had a career."

"You have me now."

"It's not enough." Diamond picked up her bags again and opened the door, "You're not enough." She knew that it would be hard to try and reposition herself back into reality, but she had to try. She couldn't live with the fact that she never knew where Jailen was or what was going on with him. She missed being a mother. She missed the life she had with Jewel. Deep down, she still loved him, but she knew that it was going to take everything in her to convince him that she was getting her life together. She wanted her family back. She knew that Jewel and Reagan were together, but she felt like Reagan was only holding her place. She couldn't live with the fact that another woman was waking up and going to sleep with Jewel and Jailen every day. As she left, Marcus sat on the end of the bed with his head in his hands. He felt his plans for him and Diamond slowly slipping through his fingers. Filled with anger, he grabbed his phone and called the person who was helping to destroy his fantasy.

"Hello?"

"What do I pay you for?" Marcus yelled into the phone.

"I know. I know. I'm taking care of it as we speak."

$$$$$

The next day, Jewel woke up with the sun shining in his face and his bed completely empty. He didn't remember falling asleep. All he remembered was taking a shower attempting to scrub the scent of hopelessness off of his body. As soon as he lay down, he was out. He had slept the rest of the night without moving a muscle. The conversation he had with Pop only added to his stress. He loved Pop like family, but he couldn't trust him at all.

"Dad, Dad, I'm late for school," Jailen said running into the room, "Hurry up and get dressed."

"J, relax, dude. I'll call your school. I was thinking you could stay home today, so we can hang out."

"But it's only 9:30 a.m."

"So that means we have all day then, huh?" Jewel said looking at the clock, "What you wanna do first?"

"Ummmm...," Jailen said throwing his backpack down on the bed, "Eat."

"As I thought," Jewel said laughing as he got out of bed, "Let me get in here and see what I can whip up." For the first time in a long time, he felt like his family was complete again.

When Jewel and Jailen got downstairs, they saw Reagan asleep on the couch.

"Ay, J, go find something to watch while I cook."

"Okay, Dad," he said excited that Jewel was home. He still missed Diamond, but for every day that she was gone, he got use to not seeing her.

Jewel walked into the kitchen and called Sacario. Now that he was out, he had some things to line up. Sacario answered on the first ring.

"Bruh, tell me a nigga is back in action?"

"What's up with you?" Jewel asked happy to hear a familiar voice.

"What's up with me? Bruh, what's up with you? You good?"

"I'm straight. You know Reagan was holding a nigga down, so I can't complain."

"What happened?"

"Diamond called me crying and shit saying that I needed to pick her up. I mean she's going through it right now, and even though we're not together anymore, I couldn't just shit on her, so I went to this white boy's house she's fucking with to get her. The dude starts tripping saying this, that, and the third, so I push the nigga to the side and walked around looking for Diamond."

"And he didn't appreciate that?"

"Shit, I guess not, so I find Diamond. She was so on. There was coke everywhere. These other bitches were in a Jacuzzi. It just wasn't a good look for D, so shit got out of hand cause Diamond was fucking ODing, and the nigga wouldn't let me take her, so me and him start fighting. He was talking about I'm not taking Diamond anywhere, so I gave it to him. The next thing I know, I'm on the ground with a gun pointed at my head, and cops stepping over me."

"That's how they had Kiko when I got back to the spot. They had lil mama in a separate room and my fucking wife on the ground with her hands cuffed behind her back. They took me all the way to the Branch, but they didn't find shit at my house, so they had to let me go. I didn't know you was down until I talked to Reagan, but that shit was a set-up fa sho. It just doesn't make sense."

"Nigga, who you telling?"

"So what, the white boy dropped the charges?"

"Shit, I don't think so. My pop's pulled a few strings for a nigga I guess."

"Wait, what?"

"Long story, bruh. Anyway, I need you to do me a favor."

"Anything, blood."

"Putting all this jail shit aside, Kisino is still living and breathing out here like it's cool, and I can't have that. I know Golden wouldn't accept me not letting every-fucking-body know that Sac belongs to M.A.C., period."

"I agree. What you need me to do?"

"I know it's short notice, but I need you to get everybody together tomorrow morning and meet me at the office. I need everybody in the same place, so I don't have to repeat myself. We all need to be on the same page, or this shit won't work."

"I got you, blood. Is that it?"

"Make sure K-2 comes with you."

"He's here with me right now."

"Alright, I'll hit you later when I have more details."

"Yep." Sacario quickly hung up the phone ready to complete his task. The M.A.C. Boys ran through his veins, so he was willing to do anything to help them all survive.

After putting on the bacon for Jailen's breakfast, Jewel left the kitchen making sure Reagan was still asleep. He had a lot of plans that he needed to put in order, but the most important one was making her his wife. When they first started dating, he knew that she was meant for him, and after everything that happened with her and Brandon, he lost hope in their relationship, but when she reappeared in his life, he knew that they were destined to be together. They had to be. After they reconnected, Jewel went out and bought her a ring. He was unsure on when or even if he wanted to give it to her, but after being away from his family for so long, and with the baby on the way, he wanted to make things right. He knew that he was going to be taking a lot of chances getting the M.A.C. Boys back to where they should have been, but being with Reagan was the only chance he cared about taking. He walked back upstairs and went into his closet. In the back was where his huge assortment of jewelry was, but in one of the drawers was a nine-carat diamond engagement ring. He pulled it out and stared at the flawlessly cut stone as it sparkled. With everything going on, Jewel wasn't too certain about his future, but if he could just spend one moment with Reagan as his wife, his life would be complete. Swallowing all of his nerves and apprehensions, Jewel tucked the ring in his pocket and made his way down the steps. When he got back downstairs, he walked into the living room and positioned himself on the couch so that Reagan was asleep lying in his arms. He admired her beauty. She was still as gorgeous as she was the first time they met. He stroked the side of her face in awe of the love he had inside for her. Reagan began to stir in her sleep from his caress.

"Hey," she said as she looked up into his eyes.

"Hey."

"Sorry I fell asleep down here. You seemed so peaceful last night, and I didn't want to wake you up." Reagan was still used to sleeping in the guestroom. Over the time that Jewel was gone, it was hard for her to sleep in their bed without him. Some nights made his absence unbearable.

"It's good," he said placing a kiss in the middle of her forehead, "You hungry?"

"Yeah, what you cooking?" Reagan asked smelling the scent of freshly cooked bacon in the air, "Did Jailen get to school okay?"

"He's in his room watching TV. I let him stay home, so we could hang out. So you know I had to cook that boy some waffles and bacon. The bacon is cooking now. It's not gon' take me long to cook the waffles."

"Sounds fun. I'll help," Reagan said trying to wobble off the couch.

"Would you relax? I got it. Plus I need to talk to you about something first."

"What is it?" The serious tone of Jewel's voice made her uneasy.

"You remember that night on the phone when I said that one day you would be my wife?"

"Yeah."

Counterfeit *Dreams 3*

Jewel got down on one knee and pulled the ring out of his pocket. "I was hoping that you would make that day today. Reagan, will you marry me?"

As soon as she saw the ring, her jaw dropped, and all she could do was put her hand over her mouth. She was speechless. Jewel remained on bended knee as she sat frozen on the couch.

"Is that a yes?" he asked in anticipation.

All Reagan could do was nod her head. She slowly extended her left hand as Jewel slid the cold, glittery ring on her finger.

"I love you so much," she screamed. She slowly stood up and wrapped her arms tightly around Jewel's neck. After everything they had been through and were still going through, Reagan just knew that marriage was only a dream for them. She had put him through hell throughout their relationship. She didn't know why she was deserving of a second chance to make things right again, but at that moment, she cherished him and their family that much more.

"You like it?" he asked noticing that she couldn't take her eyes off of the ring.

"Like it? Jewel, you have no idea how much this means to me. I know you love me, but I've hurt you so much. I just don't understand how you still do."

"You've made some mistakes in the past, but so have I. This ring is a promise that moving forward our focus will remain on each other and our family. Let's let the past be the past."

"Have you told Jailen?" she asked wanting to be as sensitive as possible.

"Not yet," he said kissing her on the lips, "Jailen."

Without hesitation, he ran into the living room. "Is the food ready?"

"Naw, not yet. Come here for a second."

Jailen sat down on the couch curious about what the excitement was about.

"J, I need to talk to you about something, and I want you to be completely honest about how you feel about it because you're a very important part of this family, okay?"

"Okay, Dad."

"Now, first I need you to know that I love your mom very much."

"I know, Dad."

"But me and your mom aren't the right people for each other. As much as I love her, we just shouldn't be in a relationship together, and that's why we don't live together anymore. We do better as friends, and I value our friendship very much, but before you and your mom moved back to Sacramento, Reagan was my girlfriend."

"So you like Reagan more than Mom?"

"No, I like Reagan differently than your mom," Jewel quickly said, "And I want you to like Reagan too."

"I do."

Reagan just smiled.

"Okay, good," Jewel said pleased with his son's maturity, "So being that I like Reagan so much, I want her to be my wife, but I want to make sure that you're okay with that first."

"So that means you guys will be married?"

"Yeah."

"So Reagan will be my mom now?" Jailen asked a little confused.

"Well…"

"Not exactly, Jailen. I would never want to or even try to replace your mom. Diamond will always be your mom, and I know she loves you very much. Our relationship will be just how it is now, but this way, you'll never be able to get rid of me," she said tickling his belly.

"So what you think, son?" Jewel asked nervous about Jailen's response.

"As long as Reagan doesn't have to cook anymore, I'm fine with it. I want you to be happy too, Daddy."

"Hey," she shot back. To her, her cooking was improving.

"When did you become so mature?" Jewel asked impressed with his son.

"I'm almost 10, Dad. Give me some credit."

"My bad, G," Jewel said laughing.

"Now if that was the big announcement, can we eat?"

"Yes, fat boy," Jewel said walking back into the kitchen as Jailen and Reagan followed closely behind him.

He was happy that things finally seemed to be coming together. As he spent time making breakfast for his family, he thanked God. He was beginning to feel like himself again. Reagan set the table as he put the finishing touches on the food, and Jailen sat on the counter and watched attentively as Jewel whisked around the kitchen.

Counterfeit *Dreams 3*

"So how's school, son?"

"It's good. I got an 'A' on my spelling quiz."

"That's what's up. Keep it up and you might just get that PlayStation 4 sooner than you thought."

Jailen couldn't help but smile from ear-to-ear. Jewel was well aware of his son's gaming addiction, but he refused for him to not have the latest and greatest of everything.

"Alright, everything's done. Go wash your hands, so we can eat."

Just as Jailen was heading toward the bathroom, the doorbell rang.

"I got it," he yelled.

"Go wash your hands, boy. I got it," Jewel said walking toward the front door.

"Morning, Jewel. Long time no see. How was County?" Detective Roberts asked with a smirk as Jewel opened it.

"What the fuck do you want?" He had to restrain himself from punching Roberts in the face.

"I came to check on you. After I heard Joe Sanchez was your father, I thought I'd come and say, 'hi.' Joe and I go way back."

"That doesn't have shit to do with me."

"Oh, but it does, Jewel. You can't rely on your father for everything, right?"

"I don't rely on him for shit. Now what do you want?"

"Consider this a courtesy visit. You were able to avoid the charges for assaulting Marcus Moore, but I don't know how a judge will feel about murder, kidnapping, and racketeering. I know that you are the head of the M.A.C. Boys organization, and I also know that you were involved in the disappearance of one Brandon Edwards. People don't just get kidnapped for no reason, Jewel. Why would anybody want to take your girlfriend?"

"Detective Roberts, right? Unless you have a warrant with you, don't show up at my house again," Jewel said slamming the door in his face.

"You'll be seeing me again very soon, Mr. Sanchez," Roberts yelled from the other side of the door, "I can promise you that."

Jewel didn't know how he knew about Brandon's death, and he wasn't concerned either. He didn't kill Brandon, so he wasn't in fear of being charged with murder, but he didn't need Roberts digging around his past either. With Golden and Will's death, and the collapse of the M.A.C. Boys, he had no time for Roberts' games.

"Is everything okay?" Reagan asked coming out of the kitchen.

"Yeah, everything is fine, babe, but can you do me a favor and make Jailen's plate?"

"Of course, you want me to make yours too?"

"Naw, I'm good right now. I gotta make a call."

Jewel ran upstairs to grab his phone. He knew that with the police snooping around, it was bad for business. He needed to nip that shit in the bud, and he knew exactly who to call.

"Ay, Pop, I need you, blood."

$$$$$

Diamond finally found enough courage to go see her mother. After leaving Marcus back at the hotel, she did her best to stay clean. She knew that it wouldn't be easy, but she was ready to get her family back. She took Jailen and Jewel for granted and regretted her decision to do so every single day. Although it may have been easier to check herself into treatment, Diamond didn't want to take the chance on Marcus being able to contact her. She would have to quit him and the drugs cold turkey. Even though he paid for everything, she made sure to keep a stash for herself since she wasn't working anymore. Being financially dependent on a man scared her, but somehow the drugs helped to ease that fear. Diamond knew that she had a long road ahead, but she was ready to begin the journey. She had to do it for her son. She reluctantly walked up to Paula's front door and rang the bell. Paula quickly answered it.

"Diamond, what are you doing here?" she asked sighing. She was glad that Jailen was back with Jewel. She was becoming use to her daughter's pop-up habits.

"Can we talk?"

Paula was tired of Diamond's excuses and sad sob stories. To her, Jailen should have been her number one priority, but slowly but surely, he wasn't. Paula was angered by Diamond's behavior because she didn't want her to make the same mistake she made by missing years out of her own child's life.

Counterfeit *Dreams 3*

"Come in." Diamond walked into the familiar house, but she felt like a stranger. "You want some water or something?" Paula asked leading her into the living room.

"No, I'm okay. Thank you."

"Well, what is it?"

Diamond gathered her words before she spoke. She wanted to make sure that she got out everything she needed to say. "How's Jailen?" she began.

"Given the circumstances, he's been better," Paula said bluntly, "But he's okay."

"Listen, Mom, I know that recently, I have been a poor excuse of a mother. There is nothing that I can say to justify my actions, and I know that. Marcus led me down a path of drugs, alcohol, excessive partying, and I happily followed behind him, but, Mom, I wasn't myself. Being a young mother prevented me from getting those tendencies out of my system early I guess, and now I'm paying the price for it. I know now that being with Marcus was only to mask the fact that I felt rejected by Jewel, and I didn't know how to handle it. Marcus made me feel good because he wanted me, or at least he pretended to want me like I pretended to want him. The drug haze he kept me in prevented me from feeling anything else, and I craved that numbness but no more. I'm not that person, and I don't want that life. I just want my family back."

"Diamond, baby, don't you think it's a little late for that?"

"No, I messed up. I can admit that now, but I know that Jewel still loves me. We have a kid together."

"He's in another relationship. I just don't want you to get your hopes up and turn back to drugs or that man for comfort."

"I know that Jewel is with Reagan, but that's only temporary. He is just hurt by what I did, but I'm gonna do whatever it takes to make sure that Jailen grows up in a home with both his mother and father."

"Diamond, you need to be focused on yourself right now."

"And I am. I want to get clean for myself, and I haven't said that before. I know that once I get my soul back, Jewel will notice the change, and we can be a family again. I miss my son."

"And what if he doesn't?"

"He will. I know Jewel. Believe me."

"So what do you want from me, Diamond?" Paula had heard her daughter's pledge to clean her life up over and over again, but for some reason, this time felt different. She saw a glimmer of Diamond's light again, and she would do whatever to help her hold onto it.

"Can I stay here?" Diamond knew that she had burned many bridges during her time with Marcus, but she needed someone to believe in her like she wanted to believe in herself.

"Do you think that's a good idea? We can find a program close by."

"No," she snapped, "I just need some time to think. If the drugs aren't being pushed in my face, I'll be okay. Honestly, my desire to get high is becoming less and less frequent because I have so much on the line. I've lost so much already. I can't imagine falling any further."

"Diamond, if I allow you to come back, I don't want you speaking or seeing that white devil."

"Mom, I've already changed my number, and he doesn't even know I'm here. Marcus doesn't mean me any good. He just has a sick fascination with me, but I'm done. I want my life back."

Paula sat quietly and thought over her daughter's proposal. As much as she was sick and tired of the drama, she was the only person Diamond had. How could she say no and turn her away? Paula pulled Diamond close to her chest and just held her. She placed a kiss on her cheek but didn't speak a word. Diamond let out every tear she held inside. She was ashamed of the person she had become, but she was determined to become better. She cried on Paula's chest for almost an hour as Paula held tightly onto her daughter. She knew that God had touched her heart, and she would do whatever was necessary to banish the demon of addiction that lived inside of her.

"We'll get through this, baby, together. I promise."

$$$$$

"It ain't nobody out here. You sure this is where they be at?"

"Jewel, for the last time, I'm sure. This definitely ain't the only trap house, but a lot of GMB niggas post up over here."

"I guess we just wait then," he said keeping an eye on the area.

After Roberts made his presence known, he knew that it was time to put his plan into action, and who better to help him than Pop. In the short amount of time that he had been a part of GMB, he picked up a lot on how they operated. He was interested in learning the ins-and-outs of the organization for his own benefit, so he paid attention to everything. When Jewel reached out to Pop for help, he knew this was his chance to prove his loyalty to Jewel.

"Here they come," he said sliding a ski mask down over his smooth chocolate face. The gun in his hand was on fire as he prepared himself for war.

The dark tint of the windows let them go unsuspected. "Ready?" Jewel asked as he followed Pop's lead and pulled his mask down.

"Ready."

In one swift motion, they got out of the car and started blasting in front of GMB's main dope house. The unregistered car that lingered in the neighborhood seemed to go unnoticed as traffic continued to flow in and out of the house. They never had any intruders in their section because after the M.A.C. Boys fell off, GMB had made a name for themselves, and they didn't expect any resistance. When they stepped out of the car, Jewel went one way and Pop went the other.

BLAT, BLAT, BLAAATTTT!

Between Jewel and Pop, it took no time to lay the niggas down in front of the house. Their bodies fell to the ground before they had a chance to reach their own guns. One of the dudes who was shot got hit in the leg. He did his best to climb up the stairs hoping to get to safety. They were the only ones there, so he could only depend on himself.

"That's Kisino's best lieutenant Robbie Segal," Pop said as he made sure the other three they shot were dead. Neighbors ran into their homes in fear of their lives, so Jewel knew it was only a matter of time before the police were called. HE walked up to Robbie and pulled him down from the stairs he tried to climb and threw him down on the concrete.

"What do you want, man? The money is in the house. Please don't kill me," Robbie said pleading for his life.

Jewel pulled up his mask exposing his face in broad day light making sure Robbie remembered him and said, "I need you to deliver a message for me. Let Kisino know that Jewel is looking for him, okay?"

Robbie looked up well aware of whom Jewel was, but he kept his mouth shut. Not pleased by Robbie's reaction, Jewel kicked him in the leg watching his blood continue to seep out. "Can you do that for me, Rob?"

"Yeah, yes, I'll tell him," Robbie winced out in pain.

"Good boy," he smirked.

"Ay, Jewel, nigga, we gotta get out of here," Pop said hearing the sound of police sirens getting louder and louder as they moved closer.

Without saying another word, he pulled his mask back down and ran to the car. Once inside, Jewel and Pop quickly removed the black hoodies and masks they had been wearing along with the black plastic that covered their shoes and threw them in a garbage bag that sat on the back seat. Jewel made his way to drop off the unregistered car knowing the police would be looking for it. He pulled up behind an abandoned building to leave the car as Pop grabbed the bag that held their clothes. Jewel had parked ten blocks down, so they slowly made their way in the opposite direction toward his Audi.

"So what do we do now?" Pop asked.

"Now we wait."

Jewel knew that killing a few of Kisino's front runners would let him know that he never had any intention of leaving, and he was ready to take back what belonged to the M.A.C. Boys. He had officially declared war.

Chapter 4

"Where is this nigga?" a guy yelled from the back of the crowded room.

"Ay yo, chill. Jewel said he'll be here, so he'll be here," Sacario said attempting to control the crowd.

After talking with Jewel, he was able to convince almost every member of the M.A.C. Boys to meet at Jewel's office to hear what he had to say. A lot of them were skeptical about his leadership, but out of respect for Golden, they came. No matter what, they were all still M.A.C. Boys even though many of them forgot what that meant.

K-2 sat patiently waiting. He wasn't officially a part of M.A.C., but whatever he could do to help, he would.

"Ay, Cari, blood, we gon' give this nigga five more minutes than we out," another man shot.

Sacario was irritated by the disrespect. Not once did anyone ever challenge Golden even when they knew he was wrong. He stood up unable to take it anymore.

"Look, I know that a lot of ya'll don't fuck with Jewel like I fuck with the nigga, and that's cool, but he is our leader. Golden would have never gone for this disrespect, and I know he would be rolling over in his grave if he knew what you niggas have become. For me, M.A.C. was never about the money or the drugs even though that comes along with the positions we each play. I was down with Golden and what he created because it was like a family. I ain't from Sac, but I knew that if I ever needed something, I could call on my brothers, and right now, Jewel needs his brothers."

"We don't owe that nigga shit," someone yelled from the crowd.

"We owe him everything...," Sacario started.

"Naw, Sacario, blood, it's good," Jewel said coming into the office with Pop following right behind him, "They're right. They don't owe me anything."

"What the fuck is he doing here?"

By this time, everyone was well aware of Pop's decision to cross over to GMB, and clique hopping was looked down upon. The room broke out into a low roar of uncertainty as they made their way to the front of the room. Pop didn't utter a word. He just kept his eyes on the floor. He couldn't bear to see the disappointment that filled each of their eyes.

"Before I start, I wanna say that if you don't feel like being here, leave. I'm not tryna waste my time or yours." No one moved a muscle. "Now, I know you all are wondering why I've asked all of you to come here. The reason is because I'm not gonna repeat what is said, and I need each and every one of you to be on the same page. For the past year and a half that I've been leading the M.A.C. Boys, I have failed you all. Golden instilled into me, Brandon, and Sacario greatness and fearlessness, but I let that slip through my fingers. I let the situation with Brandon throw me off my game, and as a result, I almost lost my family. I was so use to Golden leading me that it was easy to let him still be in the forefront making all of the decisions for me, but now that he is gone, I don't have that choice anymore. The M.A.C. Boys haven't been the same ever since Brandon left, and I want to change that, but I need you guys behind me. I know some of you may be asking why Pop is here."

Pop kept his eyes focused down on the ground.

"Despite his past transgressions, Pop is still one of us. I know it's hard, but we must all forgive him. I wonder sometimes if I would have tried to reach out to Brandon would things have turned out differently. It's too late to know now, but it's not too late for Pop. I won't forget him. I'm reaching out."

Sacario was a little skeptical about Pop's presence, but in an act of solidarity, he got up and stood next to him. K-2 followed suit.

"The M.A.C. Boys can be as strong as ever if we can come together and make this shit work. It's war out here, and if we don't fall in line, niggas might not make it to next week."

Pop finally spoke up, "I know that a lot of ya'll don't give a fuck about what I have to say, but Kisino isn't gonna stop until we're all dead especially after today."

"It pains me to see the clique in shambles like this. Kisino's been plotting on M.A.C. before Golden even stepped down. He wanted war, so that's what we're gonna give him. GMB has a trap house off Valley Hi. Me and Pop hit up the spot and knocked a few niggas down, but we let Kisino's front runner know that the M.A.C. Boys never left and don't intend to. This is our city. A lot of shit is gon' come from this, so if this ain't what you want, leave now cause I can't have anybody else's blood on my hands. You niggas are like my brothers, and it's my job to make sure you get money, so that's the shit I'm on now. No more bullshit."

Jewel hoped that his words resonated with his team. He knew Pop would be a hard sell, but he couldn't turn his back on him.

"We're in this together, Jewel."

"M.A.C. or nothing."

Members of the crew started to get hyped as they were reminded of how things used to be. Golden was a martyr to them, and they couldn't let his life be in vain.

"Smackz, what's up with the trap?" Jewel asked Golden's youngest nephew.

Ever since GMB flooded their product throughout Sacramento, the M.A.C. Boys were seen few and far between, and a result, their profits completely dried up.

"I mean we're still good on work, but ain't nobody pushing shit," Smackz said adjusting his glasses.

"Not anymore. Packs need to be pushed now. I want to draw as much attention to ourselves as we can."

"What about the boys?"

"You let me worry about that, blood. Now if you were on the frontline, I need you to hook up with Smackz and get your quota. Smackz, give everybody what they need. If niggas been in a drought then I want it to flood. We need more bodies on the streets. Kisino ain't gon' take the competition lightly, so until I say otherwise, nigga, it's shoot first. Period."

For the rest of the meeting, Jewel made sure that everyone knew what position to play. They had to be ready.

$$$$$

Kisino sat back in his chair with a cigar in his mouth counting a pile of hundreds that lay across his desk. He took pride in leading GMB to domination. He had accomplished everything he wanted, and with Jewel completely out of the picture, he forgot all about Pop. Letting them live was the least he could do after he stopped their money flow and killed Golden. He felt like he had gotten rid of the source of the problem. He continued to count each bill with joy in his heart. It was the only thing he cared about. Suddenly, Blue, Kisino's business partner, busted into the room holding Robbie up by his shoulders. Blood trailed them with each step they took. Blue threw him down on the chair as he ripped Robbie's shirt from off of his body and tied it tightly around his leg.

"What the fuck happened?" Kisino yelled. There had been peace in paradise for months, so he was confused.

"He got shot," Blue spoke up.

"I can see that, nigga. What the fuck happened, Robbie?"

He screamed out in pain as Blue recklessly poured a bottled of rubbing alcohol onto the gaping wound and continued to strangle his leg with the shirt. Once he finished, Robbie was able to speak.

"Man, me, Tone, Mark, and Dash were posted off Valley Hi. Shit was running cool at first, but then this black Nissan pulled up down the block, but we didn't think nothing of it. We start busting knocks here and there, but the car never moved. I should've known something was up. Before we knew it, two niggas masked up, ran out of the car, and started blasting. They hit Tone and Mark first. Their bodies slumped to the ground before they got to Dash. Dash tried to run to the back of the house, but one of the bullets hit him in the back then the other nigga shoots me in the leg. I tried to go back into the house, but one of them pulled me from off the stairs and threw me on the ground. He pulled off his mask and told me to tell you that Jewel is looking for you."

Kisino remained silent at the mention of Jewel's name. He had to admit that he was impressed because he thought that he was just one of Golden's puppets. He got excited about the possibility of finishing the M.A.C. Boys off for good. It was no fun for him if they weren't going to fight back.

"So everybody's dead?" Kisino asked adjusting his golden-wire frames.

"The ambulance took Dash to the hospital. I overheard them say that Tone and Mark are dead though," Robbie said staring at the ground.

"Blue, do me a favor and see if you can find out anything about Dash."

"Got it," he said walking out of the room. When he opened the door, a small Dominican chick with a big butt, smooth golden brown skin, and jet-black hair rushed past him.

62

Counterfeit *Dreams 3*

"Kisino, we need to talk," she said in a thick, Spanish accent.

"Asaya, shawty, this is not a good time. Let me get with you later. I have a situation right now," he said pointing to Robbie.

"I don't give two fucks. We need to talk now," Asaya said crossing her arms across her chest.

"Give me a sec," Kisino said to Robbie as he pulled her out into the hallway. "I told you that I would call you." Asaya was a little more demanding and entitled than he had initially thought.

"And you didn't, so now I'm here."

"Well, now that you're here, how can I help you?"

"You promised me that Jewel would be dead for what he did to my cousin, but the last that I heard, he's walking around a free man without a care in the mothafucking world."

Brandon had been in contact with Kisino after he and Jewel fell out, and Kisino assured him that he would be in charge once Kisino took over the M.A.C. Boys. He had convinced Brandon that he was a stakeholder in the organization, and that after Golden stepped down, M.A.C. would naturally fall in his hands. Kisino manipulated Brandon and fueled the hate that began to form for Jewel, so when Golden announced Jewel as his successor, he lost it. He wanted Jewel's head by any means, so he and Kisino kept in touch as they plotted on Jewel's downfall and GMB's takeover.

Asaya and Brandon were very close. He didn't have any siblings of his own, but she was the closest thing he had to a sister. After his mother died from cancer, his aunt and uncle encouraged him to come and stay with them and Asaya, but by that time, the streets had a tight grip on him. Despite him declining their offer, he and Asaya stayed in contact. When he first found out that she was stripping and later prostituting herself, he was happy that she was about her money. He never judged her for what she did because he knew they were cut from the same cloth. When Brandon sent Robyn to stay with her, she did her best to mold Robyn into the woman he had requested her to be. Asaya thought that she had adjusted to the lifestyle and had become comfortable selling her body for money until she found Robyn floating in a pool of her own blood. Asaya never imagined her taking her own life, but she couldn't understand why he was so disconnected from the situation when she told him that Robyn was dead. His calmness throughout the whole process scared her, and his behavior became so erratic. After not hearing from him for several weeks after Robyn's funeral, she went to his house to find him. He was family, and that meant everything to her. She would do anything to protect him. Asaya knocked on the door but received no answer, so she used her spare key to let herself in hoping to find anything that would give her some sort of answers and lead her to Brandon, but she found nothing. After searching the place high and low, Asaya decided to leave praying for her cousin's safety with each step she took. When she arrived back to her car, she realized that she left her phone in the car. She had one missed call. It was from Brandon. The blinking voicemail icon sent a sense of relief throughout her body. She hurried to listen to the voicemail.

"Hey, cuz, I'm on my way to your house now. I've been trying to call you, but you ain't answering. Just know that I'm on my way," he kept repeating, "My phone is about to die, so if I don't make it, I stopped by Jewel's. I love you, cuz."

Asaya was more confused than before. She knew about Brandon and Jewel's fallout, so the message didn't make sense. She didn't know that those would be the last words she would ever hear from her cousin. She went back into the house as she continued to call his cell, but he never picked up. She wouldn't be able to leave with a good conscience until she found him, so she waited for hours, but Brandon never answered. She didn't know for sure, but deep down, she knew that he was dead. While she sat alone crying for the loss of her cousin, she heard a phone ringing in his bedroom. She hurried to answer the small black phone praying that it was Brandon, but it was Kisino. She knew that he and Kisino did business together from time-to-time, but she didn't know the full extent of their relationship. Kisino confirmed Asaya's suspicions, and after talking to him, she couldn't do anything but blame Jewel and Golden for Brandon's disappearance. After speaking with Kisino, she had no other choice but to go to him for guidance. She wanted Jewel's head, and he intended to grant her that wish. When Asaya returned home, she stopped working because she couldn't think of anything other than making Jewel pay for what he did to Brandon. Her on-again off-again girlfriend Veronica was worried about her depressive state. She wanted Asaya to stop hoeing because it was something that they always fought about, so when she saw how Brandon's disappearance affected her, she wanted to help in any way she could. She knew how much he meant to Asaya, so she was willing to do whatever to give her girlfriend peace of mind even if that meant jeopardizing her own career. Veronica worked for the Sacramento Police Department and had convinced Detective Roberts to pursue Jewel after Diamond was kidnapped and investigate into the case further. She needed him to make the connection tying Jewel to Brandon's disappearance, but Jewel's hands were clean. Not willing to wait for justice to be served the legal way, Asaya took the law into her own hands. She linked up with Kisino because she believed that he was the only one who would be able to kill Jewel. Since he felt the need to flex, Kisino hoped for her sake that Asaya would finally make herself useful.

"Listen, shawty, those things take time. I'ma very particular man, you know?"

"Kisino, it has been months, and my cousin is still nowhere to be found. You know like I know that Jewel had something to do with it."

"I agree."

"So what do you plan on doing about it?"

"Nothing. We sit and wait. We let Jewel come to us, baby girl."

"No lo creo. If you won't help me, fine, but I promise you that nigga will pay for what he did to my cousin. Believe that."

Without saying another word, Asaya left impatiently leaving Kisino behind to sit and wait for his plan to unfold right before her eyes.

$$$$$

Reagan sat in the middle of the living room floor with bridal magazines surrounding her. Her belly made it hard for her to move around, but that didn't stop her from planning the wedding of her dreams. She researched different venues, cakes, dresses, hairstyles, honeymoon destinations. Everything had to be perfect. After she cheated on Jewel with Brandon, she never imagined that he would ever be able to forgive her let alone make her his wife. She felt so undeserving of him, but her love for him transcended their past mistakes. She was ready to spend the rest of her life with him. She was almost due, and the thought of her and Jewel's families coming together made the idea of marriage and motherhood a little less scary.

Sasha Ravae

She was excited to meet her son despite the circumstances. She had forgiven herself for what happened, and she refused to blame her unborn child for the actions of her or Brandon. She began to rub her round belly at the thought.

As Reagan continued to flip through the pages of various magazines, she felt even more insecure about her body. The extra weight she was carrying around was foreign for her. She began contemplating on whether she should start planning for the wedding before or after she had the baby. She had a vision of herself at her wedding, and that vision didn't include being pregnant in a white gown. Despite her fantasy wedding, being married to Jewel meant everything to her. The way things were going, she would have just been happy getting married at the court house. She looked around the living room at the various cut-outs and felt silly. It was all too much pressure.

"We'll just plan it later," she said to herself as she gathered up her wedding books. Just as she was about to throw all of the preparations she had made away, her phone rang. It was Jewel. "Hey, baby," Reagan sang into the phone, "I was just thinking about you."

"You miss me?"

"Of course I do. I feel like I haven't really seen you since you got home."

"I know, and that's my fault. I have a lot I have to take care of before we get married."

"Jewel, we haven't even set a date yet."

"So? It's gonna be soon though, right?" he questioned.

"I was thinking about the whole big wedding thing, and I think I changed my mind."

"About?"

"About everything. I love you more than life itself, and I want to be your wife, but with the baby coming, I just feel like it's just bad timing. I think we should get married at the courthouse," she said plainly.

"Courthouse? Reagan, isn't this gonna be your first marriage?"

"Yes."

"Isn't this mine?"

"Yeah."

Counterfeit *Dreams 3*

"Okay then. I'm not getting married at no mothafucking courthouse."

"But, Jewel..."

"But, nothing. What's really up, Rea?"

"I mean I'm 8-months, and I'm huge, Jewel. I've gained at least fifty pounds. I know it sounds superficial or whatever, but when I imagined my wedding day, I didn't imagine myself looking like a whale."

"Reagan, you sound ridiculous," Jewel laughed.

"Jewel, I'm serious. I want the big wedding, but just not like this."

"How much time do you need? Six months? A year? What?"

"At least that."

"Okay then, we'll plan to have it a year from now. Will that be better?"

"Yes and no. I want us to be married now," she whined.

"Reagan, we gotta have some give and take here. I'm not going anywhere. A year is a reasonable amount of time. I don't want you to rush this, babe. Whatever you want that's what you're gonna get. The baby will almost be a year old by that time; you can start working out, all the shit. Don't sacrifice your dreams out of convenience, okay?"

"Okay." Reagan said staring down at her wedding books elated that Jewel had convinced her to wait.

"Perfection takes time."

"You're prefect."

"Far from it," he laughed.

He knew that things were shaky when it came to the M.A.C. Boys, but he had to make sure things were right at home. He made a promise to Reagan that he intended to keep.

Ding. Dong.

"Who's that?" Jewel asked hearing the doorbell in the background.

"I ordered some food."

"Then you wonder why you're getting fat."

"Shut up. I'm hungry."

"Well, I'll let you get to it. Kiss Jailen for me."

"I let him spend the night at Jalil's house. He'll be back in the morning. I'll have him call you?" she asked hoping that he was coming home.

"Yeah, do that. I'ma be working late, but I'll hit you when I know something."

By this time, Reagan knew what Jewel's work entailed, but she had to let him be a man and handle his business.

"I love you, Jewel. Please be careful."

"Ain't I always?"

"Bye."

Ding. Dong. Ding. Dong. Ding. Dong. Ding. Dong.

The person at the door became more impatient with each second that passed. "Hold on, I'm coming," Reagan yelled. She pulled out her money as she opened the door.

"Reagan?"

Reagan put her hands up as Asaya aimed a gun to her head. Asaya couldn't believe that nobody was there for Brandon not even the woman he loved. She looked down at her belly noticing the life growing inside. Reagan was frozen.

"After all that Brandon did for you, this is how you repay my cousin, puta?" Asaya asked as she brushed past Reagan into the house with the gun still pointed at her head, "Where is he?"

"Where is who?"

Reagan hadn't seen Asaya in over a year, and the times she did, it was only in passing. She didn't even know Asaya knew who she was.

"Jewel," she screamed.

"Asaya, please calm down. Jewel isn't here, okay? It's just me. Can you put the gun down? We can talk about this."

"Fuck talking, mami. I'm gonna kill Jewel just like he did Brandon. Now where is he?"

"Asaya, I promise you Jewel is not here."

Asaya became frustrated at the sound of Reagan's voice. She didn't believe a word she said. To her, they all had plotted against Brandon, and she was there to make things right again. Asaya slammed the butt of the gun on the side of Reagan's face, and blood splattered across the carpet as she fell to the ground. As blood seeped from the side of her face, all she could think about was protecting her child.

"Please don't hurt my baby," Reagan said with her head down, "I don't know what you want with Jewel, but he's not here."

Counterfeit *Dreams 3*

"Do you think I give a fuck about that bastard's baby? My cousin loved you, and you betray him by getting pregnant by the enemy? Bitch, you're dirt," Asaya spat.

"It's Brandon's."

"What did you say?" she asked as she pointed the gun back at Reagan's head.

"The baby is Brandon's. I got pregnant by Brandon," she hurried to say.

"Do you expect me to believe that?"

"Believe what you want, but this is Brandon's son. I'm 8-months."

Asaya lowered the gun as she stared at Reagan's stomach. She couldn't harm her own bloodline. She was happy to know that his legacy would continue, but there were still a lot of questions that needed to be answered.

"Where is he?"

"Honestly, I don't know. It's been so long since I've talked to him. I just assumed…"

"That he's dead?"

"I don't know what else to think."

"Your baby's father goes missing, and you didn't think to call the police?"

"And say what? Brandon had his own demons. He crossed a lot of people, but I know that Jewel didn't have anything to do with it," Reagan lied, "I think about him every day. I think about how our son will never know his father, and I'm the one who's gonna have to explain that."

"Why Jewel?"

"Me and Jewel were together before me and Brandon. Even though I cared about him, I never stopped loving Jewel, but that's my fault for leading Brandon on, and now I'm paying the consequences for it. Believe me."

Asaya was even more confused than before. As much as she wanted Jewel dead, she couldn't imagine harming Reagan or her family's blood that coursed through the baby's veins to get to Jewel, so she left without saying anything else leaving Reagan sitting on the floor as blood continued to seep from her face.

$$$$$

Sasha Ravae

Jewel remained at the office after everyone left. He had to make sure that they were all on point because the next few weeks would be hell. Word spread fast that M.A.C. had made their presence known again, and their first target was GMB. Jewel purposely left Robbie alive. He wanted him to go back and let Kisino know that he wasn't willing to just lie down. Despite Golden's death, he had an obligation to all of his potnahs. Certain circumstances made him appear weak, but he was ready to show the world why he was crowned king of his city. He sat at his huge mahogany wood desk and reminisced on all the times he had spent with Brandon and Golden there. Sometimes his loneliness consumed him, but he had to remain focused. As he became lost in his thoughts, his office phone rang.

"Hello?" he answered unsure of the number.

"Well, there he is," Kisino said applauding into the phone, "I thought I would find you there since you call yourself being on some boss shit all of a sudden. I guess Golden taught you something, huh?"

"What you calling me for?" As far as Jewel was concerned, he was done talking to Kisino. He knew there would be no reasoning with him, so at that point he was ready to let his guns talk for him.

"I'm ready to talk, Jewel. Being that you shot up my boys and almost bodied two, I thought we should square shit away. You let me know when's a good time for you, young blood."

"Ain't no talking going on, Kisino blood. You know where to find me, and best believe I know where to find you too, but I'ma let you decide on whether you leave Sac peacefully, or if I'ma lay you and your whole clique out one bullet at a time. You might have had Golden shook, but I'm not that nigga. Remember that."

"Such big words from such a little nigga," Kisino said laughing, "Okay, Jewel, I'll play along, but don't say that I didn't try to give you a way out." *Click.* He hung up excited by the cat and mouse game. He wanted full control of the M.A.C. Boys, but taking it from Jewel's cold dead hands would satisfy him even more. Robbie's leg wound was healing by the day, but Kisino barely gave him any time to rest before he was back on the streets. Dash was lucky enough to only receive a flesh wound. When he was in the hospital, the fact that he didn't have any insurance came up, so against medical advice, he split leaving only bloody bandages behind. He heard about the war between GMB and M.A.C., so despite the pain, he was back at it with Robbie and the rest of GMB.

Jewel sat back and knew at that moment, there was nothing he could say to stop what was about to happen. He just prayed that his soldiers were ready. As he gathered his stuff and headed out the door to meet with Sacario, he ran right into K-2.

"Thank God I found you, nigga," he said out of breath.

"What's up? Where you coming from?"

"I was on my way to the trap, but I noticed this black Charger following me. I mean I was going hella out the way, but the mothafucka stayed on my ass."

"You didn't bring them over here, did you?"

"Fuck naw. It was an undo fa sho. I couldn't see into the car, but only the boys do weird-ass shit like that. I parked like three blocks down then I cut to the back and came up the stairs."

Jewel knew that it could only be Roberts. For whatever reason, it was like he had a hard-on for him, and he knew that if he and K-2 were being watched then the rest of the M.A.C. Boys were too.

"Stay right here, blood." Jewel pulled out his cell phone and called Sacario.

"Hello?" he asked answering on the first ring.

"Ay, what's up with it? Where you at?"

"Shit, I just linked up with Pop. We was about to blast out to the North. Why, what's up?"

"K-2 came by the office and said that an undercover was following him for the past couple hours, so be cool. Ya'll might as well go post up or something. I'll hit you back when I know more."

"Got you."

Jewel was frustrated by Roberts' persistence. He didn't understand what his fascination was with him, but he had to figure it out fast. He had no time to waste.

"Where's Sacario at?"

"He said him and Pop were on their way to the North."

"They need to cancel that fast. It's hotter than wasabi out here, blood. What's really going on?"

"I don't know, but I intend on finding out. I'll get at you though," Jewel said as he headed towards the door again. All he could think about was getting back home to Reagan.

Sasha Ravae

"Where you bout to go?" K-2 questioned.

"To the spot. Why, what's up?"

"I mean the way shit is going right now, the house might be the last place you wanna go. I just don't think you wanna draw attention to the home front, feel me?"

"Where you going?"

"To see Gabby."

"Exactly, I'm tryna see my bitch too."

"Just slide over there with me. We can talk to Joe. Maybe he heard something. I mean we ain't all on the radar for some domestic dispute shit, blood. It gotta be bigger than that."

As much as Jewel didn't want to be around his father, he agreed to go with K-2. He had a few more questions for Joe to answer. They decided to leave in separate cars. If the police were following them, Jewel didn't want them to be seen together. Roberts was well aware that Joe was Jewel's father, so he felt like he might finally be able to use that to his benefit.

K-2 got into his car and headed towards Gabrielle's. It had been a few weeks since he'd seen her, and with everything going on, he really missed her.

"Hey," he said answering on the first ring.

"You on your way?"

"Yeah, I just had to stop by Jewel's, but I'm on my way now."

"Why'd you have to see Jewel?"

"Because I had to talk to him about something, Gabby. Chill."

"I was just asking."

"Anyway, he's following me over there now."

"For what?" she asked becoming defensive. She was relieved that Joe was able to get him out of jail, but she knew how he felt about their father, and she wanted to protect him.

"Gabby, cut it out."

"I think I have the right to ask, Keith."

"Look, we'll talk about it when we get there. Bye."

K-2 loved Gabrielle, but his loyalty would always remain with Sacario and his clique, so he tried to stay clear of the Sanchez family disputes. Fifteen minutes later, he pulled up in front of Gabrielle's house. After making sure Jewel was following close behind, K-2 directed him to park in the driveway. Jewel reluctantly got out of the

72

car as he stared at his father's house. It was nothing compared to what they used to have. The home didn't even seem like it would appeal to Joe, but Jewel had to remind himself that he didn't know him anymore.

"Ay, I'm not tryna be here all day," he shot.

"I got you, blood. We just gon' talk to Joe for a sec, and then we can dip. I know that he seems like he's out the loop, but that nigga knows more than he lets on. We can't move forward with the boys following our every move anyway."

Jewel didn't say anything. He knew K-2 was right, but the thought of being around his father again put his stomach in knots. K-2 walked to the door and rang the doorbell as Jewel stayed behind feeling like he wanted to run the other way, but his pride made him stay still. A couple of seconds later, the door opened.

"Hi, Keith, what are you doing here?"

"Hey, Ms. Isabella, I just came by to see Gabby for a minute, and I needed to speak with Joe too. Is he home?"

"Yeah, he's in his office," she said never taking her eyes off of Jewel. Even though so many years had passed, she could never forget his face. There was a big piece of Joe inside of him that was undeniable.

K-2 walked into the house hoping Gabrielle or Joe would come and tear him away from the awkward silence but no one came. "Have you met Jewel?" he asked hoping to get the conversation started.

"A very long, long time ago. Hi, Jewel, I'm Isabella. It's very nice to see you again," she said extending her hand toward Jewel's. He accepted it, but the feeling was not mutual. He finally got to look into the eyes of the woman who broke up his family, and he still despised her. Isabella could sense Jewel's hesitation. She wanted him to feel welcomed, but she didn't want to push the issue. "Let me go grab your father."

Hearing the conversation from the other room, Gabrielle ran to meet K-2. She missed him like crazy.

"Baby," she squealed.

K-2 wrapped his long arms tightly around her waist, lifting her tiny frame off the ground. "What's up babe?"

As they continued to display their affections for each other, Joe made his way downstairs. He didn't believe that Jewel was really there when Isabella told him, but he was excited to see his son outside of jail.

"Jewel, can I talk to you?" He didn't want to waste any more time.

"Me and Keith will be in the back," Gabrielle said hoping to use Jewel's presence as a distraction.

"Keep the door open," Isabella yelled.

Jewel followed Joe into his office closing the door behind him. "Have a seat." Joe sat at his desk and stared at Jewel as he sat uncomfortably waiting for him to speak. "Now what do I owe this surprise?"

"K-2 said he needed to talk to you. I just came along."

"Well, now that you're here, I think that this would be a good time for us to talk, don't you think?"

"What is there to talk about?"

"Everything. Jewel, you can't keep running away from me. Even though you don't want to doesn't stop me from wanting to be a part of you and Jailen's lives. I've made many mistakes, and I have suffered because of it, but I want to make things right."

"Don't use me to clear your fucking conscience. I appreciate you pulling whatever strings you did, but that's as far as it goes. I'm not gon' pretend like the past twelve years never existed. I can't pretend."

"And I don't expect you to."

"Well, what do you want from me?"

"A chance to be your father, a father that you deserve."

"I don't need a father. The only man who looked out for me is dead. I'm my own man now, and I don't want your help."

"Jewel, it hurts me every day that you're willing to put your life and freedom on the line just to belong to something bigger than yourself. Your mother and I were your family. We should have been there for you. We should have been there to protect you."

"But you weren't, but I was able to maintain on my own. I found my family."

Joe was devastated by the path that Jewel decided to take. He had envisioned so much more for his son, and he couldn't help but blame himself for how his life turned out.

"I understand why you did what you did. I just feel like I failed you, but you are who you are today because of what you had to endure. I just don't want you to be put in a predicament that you may not be able to get yourself out of."

"That's what I have money for, right? You taught me that, Dad," Jewel shot back, "I don't need you tryna lecture me. You made millions getting criminals off every day, but I guess it's different when it's your own son, huh?"

"I've changed, Jewel. Money is not everything to me anymore. I was blinded by what it can do for you because I never knew any different. I never had to struggle. Everything has always been handed to me including your mother. I never loved Laura, but the agreement that our families came to didn't take that into consideration. It was seen as a sacrifice on my part. It was only about what could be gained from our unholy union. The only thing that I do thank God for is you. The money, the house, the cars mean nothing to me."

Joe had always lived his life extravagantly, but after he quit being a defense attorney, he found unknown peace in the simple things. All the things he had taken for granted like being a good father and husband now meant everything. Jewel sat back and let his words sink in. He had to admit that he didn't recognize the man sitting in front of him. The cold, disconnected, money obsessed man he had grown up with seemed to be no more. Jewel couldn't deny that not having his mother and father in his life left a hole inside of him, but he had been empty for so long that he didn't know anything else. He didn't know if he even wanted the void to be filled.

"What do you expect me to do?"

"Let me be there. I know that it's not going to happen overnight, but we can fix things if we try. I want Jailen to know who Gabrielle and I are. I don't want to be strangers to you guys anymore. You're angry, and you have every right to be, but let me fix this."

Jewel had carried around the burden of hate and resentment around for Joe for what seemed like a lifetime. The anger that he held in his heart became a part of who he was. How could he just let it go?

"Jailen's mom is having a hard time right now, so being around family," Jewel struggled to say, "would probably be good for him."

"Diamond, right?"

"Yeah, how'd you know?"

"I looked more into your file, and I spoke with a few people, and all my leads pointed me to Detective Roberts."

"That's the mothafucka that arrested me."

"I know. I guess when Diamond and Jailen were kidnapped, your name came up more than once."

"They think I would kidnap my own son? For what?"

"No, but the police think that it was retaliatory. Being in the type of work you're in that's not so uncommon. When Diamond and her boyfriend Marcus became involved, his parents were against it, but being as rebellious as he is, Marcus continued to see her, and that's why you were held in jail for longer than was necessary for the charges against you because Marcus wanted you out of the picture for good. And with Roberts grabbing for straws, he was hoping to pin something else on you to keep you locked up because they knew the assault and trespassing charges were bullshit, excuse my language, especially with Diamond's corroboration of your story."

"What about now? I don't even talk to Diamond."

"What's going on now?"

"The police have been following me, K-2, and my whole clique. We can't make a move without being tailed."

"I haven't heard anything else," Joe said scratching his head, "They are really out to get you."

"So what the fuck do I do?"

"Nothing. Stay low. They can't get you on anything if you don't give them anything."

"I can't promise that," Jewel said staring Joe in his eyes.

"Jewel, you need to be smart."

"And I am. There's a war going on out there that you have no idea about. Niggas are dying every day, and if I'm not smart, I could be next. I don't have time to wait for shit to die down."

"What about Jailen?"

"What about Jailen?" Jewel tensed up at the sound of his son's name. Even though it didn't seem like it, everything he was doing was for him.

"If he's at home while you're out here, who's watching him?"

"I appreciate your concern, Joe, but he's fine. He's at home with my girlfriend Reagan."

"Jewel, I know that you have a lot going on right now, and I want to help you as much as I can. With Reagan being pregnant, how about Jailen comes and stays here until things are situated. I know that you can take care of him, but for their sake, it would be no problem for me and Isabella to keep him for a few days. We live not that far from you, so taking him to school will be no problem. I just want to help, Jewel."

Joe was more than concerned for Jewel and Jailen's safety, and he wanted to prove to Jewel that he could be there for him as a father should. He had to show that he wasn't the same man anymore even if it killed him.

"Let me talk to Reagan," he said reluctantly.

"That's all I can ask you to do," Joe said smiling.

$$$$$

After receiving the call from Jewel, Sacario and Pop abandoned their plans to go and meet up with Golden's nephew Smackz. They had a full day of checking dope spots and collecting money, but with the police tailing them, they decided against it.

"So what do we do now?" Pop asked as he busted a U-turn.

"Just drive around I guess," Sacario said.

This was the first time that they were working directly with each other, and as much Sacario wanted to let go of the fact that Pop was a part of Golden's death for the sake of Jewel and the M.A.C. Boys, he couldn't.

"What made you come back?"

The question caught Pop off guard. He knew that he would have to answer for what he did, so he felt like he owed Sacario an explanation.

"My loyalty to Jewel. I made a mistake, and I know that. If I could bring Will and Golden back, I would in a heartbeat. I know that even though I didn't pull the trigger myself, I might as well have. I can't say that shit wouldn't of happened without me, but I didn't help the situation, and now their blood will forever be on my hands. Despite all that, I couldn't let the same thing happen to Jewel. I owe him everything."

"After all the M.A.C. Boys did for you, why was it so easy to switch up like that?" Sacario asked out of curiosity as he rolled a blunt. He tried not to judge Pop, but trusting his motives was proving harder than he thought.

"It wasn't easy, blood. Before I hooked up with Brandon and Jewel, I was invisible to you niggas, but when I started laying niggas out and putting in work with no hesitation then I became one of you. I didn't want to lose that."

"Pop, you always were one of us. We all play different parts to keep this shit popping. Some nigga's jobs is to be in the front not because they're better, but because they play a different position, but that don't make us better than somebody who's playing the back."

"It didn't seem like that. After Brandon shot me, I know that my mind should have been on getting better, or maybe getting ready for school or something, but it wasn't. All I could think about was money and how to get it. It didn't register when Jewel said K-2 was taking my place. Not after everything I had done to be where I was."

"K-2 was just like you. He was just tryna get in where he fit in. Believe me."

"It's in the past I guess. All I can do now is move forward, feel me? I know niggas ain't fucking with me, bruh, and I don't blame them, but M.A.C. is in my blood. I'd die for this shit."

"I can't say that I understand why you did what you did, but I do understand wanting to make a name for yourself, and you definitely managed to do that."

"Nigga, who you telling? I know it's only a matter of time before Kisino comes looking for me, so I gotta beat him to it."

As Sacario and Pop continued to circle around the city, the unidentified car that was following them never missed a beat. At this point, the car wasn't trying to be inconspicuous anymore. Roberts wanted to be in plain sight.

"Is that undo still following us?"

"Hell yeah, blood," Pop said looking out the rearview mirror.

Roberts continued to follow behind Sacario and Pop hoping they would lead him to Jewel. He had all of his team out in the streets trailing every known M.A.C. Boy and anyone they were associated with, but each time they came up with nothing. Jewel couldn't afford them to, but Roberts was desperate. Marcus had been hounding him ever since he found out that Jewel was released from jail. His family had invested a lot of money into Roberts, so Marcus expected results. Without him being able to get ahold of Diamond, he was going crazy. In his own twisted way, he loved her. He was just unable to show it. Jewel and his team were giving Roberts nothing to work with, but to get Jewel off the streets for good, he needed something solid. As Roberts continued to follow behind Sacario and Pop, his phone rang.

"Allyn, it's been a few days now, and I haven't received any good news," Marcus shouted into the phone, "What the fuck is my family paying you for?"

"Believe me, Marcus, I'm working as hard as I can."

"You efforts are not appreciated, Allyn. For $100,000, I expected Jewel Sanchez handed to me on a fucking silver platter."

"In a perfect world," Roberts laughed nervously.

"My world is perfect."

"Marcus, I just need a little more time."

"Time's up. Meet me downtown in twenty minutes. I'm ready to finish this once and for all."

Chapter 5

Asaya sat on the couch spaced out from the lines of coke she continued to fill her nose with. She was numb. She wanted her mind to turn off, but the thought of Brandon's baby growing inside of Reagan killed her because she knew her cousin wouldn't see his son grow up, but she had to be there. She was the last link the baby would have to their family, and she couldn't sacrifice that. Brandon would have wanted her to protect his seed. Asaya let the effects of the drugs soothe her mind for the time being. As she continued to stew in her thoughts, the front door opened, but she didn't even have the energy to turn around and see who it was.

"Hey, baby, what are you doing here?" Veronica asked as she walked around the couch to sit down. Asaya didn't say anything as her tears continued to line her cheeks. "Baby, what's wrong?" Veronica asked as she wiped the tears that fell. She softly planted a kiss on Asaya's face leaving her concern lightly on her skin.

"I know that after everything that nigga has done, he should have a bullet hole in his face, but with Reagan being pregnant, how can I do that?"

"First, no bullet should be anywhere. I told you me and Roberts are handling this case, so just let the police do their job, okay, Saya?"

"Where the fuck has that gotten me? I don't expect you to understand. All you hear is that the cops are here to protect and serve, but you and I both know that's bullshit."

"Asaya, please…" As Veronica tried to console Asaya's doubtful spirit, her phone rang. "It's work, baby. Hold on," she said as she answered her work phone, "Hello?"

"Veronica Matthews?"

"This is she. How can I help you?"

"I have information about Jewel Sanchez."

Veronica couldn't believe her luck. Her love for Asaya made her desperate to bring Brandon's killer to justice. Asaya said that it was Jewel, so it had to be him, and Veronica was determined to make him pay.

"Asaya, hand me that pen over there," she said with her hand covering the phone. In a daze, she slowly grabbed the pen from the coffee table and handed it to Veronica.

Counterfeit *Dreams 3*

"Okay and your name?" Veronica asked ready to pursue the new lead.

"None of that is relevant. I need to speak with Detective Roberts. I was just hoping that you could help with that."

"Roberts is unavailable at this time, but I can assure you that I will get your information to him."

"No, it's either I talk to Roberts, or I don't talk at all."

"Roberts is not available," Veronica repeated.

"I have information about the death of Brandon Edwards. I think he can make time to speak to me."

Veronica lost her breath at the sound of Brandon's name. She knew that Jewel had something to do with his death, but she could never make the connection.

"How do I know that you're a reliable source?"

"You don't, but Roberts will. I'll be expecting a call from him. You have one hour." *Click.*

"Hey, baby, I gotta go, but I will be back. This is going to end soon, okay? I promise," Veronica said placing her soft pink lips on Asaya's, "I'll call you later. Please stay here til I get back. I love you." She was used to Asaya's disappearing acts. They had become frequent in their relationship, but now she was more worried than ever. Asaya barely noticed Veronica's presence as the drugs clouded her mind. All she could think about was Reagan.

Veronica ran out to her car quickly trying to dial Roberts' number. For the past few months, they had been grasping at straws trying to find something to use against Jewel, but she knew he was guilty.

"Hey, V, this is a bad time. Let me call you back, okay?"

"Detective Roberts, listen. I got a lead on the Sanchez case. An informant stated that he had information linking Sanchez to the Edwards disappearance, but he stated that he would only talk to you."

"I don't have time right now. I need you to take the lead on this, Veronica."

"Sir, that's not possible, the informant made it very clear that either he talks to you or he walks, and we can't afford that. Whatever leads we get, we need to utilize them. Jewel Sanchez is a free man while my girlfriend's cousin is still yet to be found. I know that there's a conflict of interest here, sir, but it is very important that we solve this case."

"What's this guy's information?" Roberts asked breaking down. He had a soft spot for Veronica, and he respected her work ethic and how she was able to climb the ranks to become a junior detective in such a short amount of time.

"He didn't give me a name. All I have is a number."

"I'm ready."

"752-6347."

"I'll call you if anything comes up."

"Thank you, Detective. I'll be at the station."

"Bye, Veronica."

Roberts parked at the spot Marcus had requested, but he was nowhere in sight. As he waited, he looked down at the number he had gotten from Veronica. So far all of his leads had led him in circles. He was skeptical about the newfound information, but he decided to entertain the tip anyway.

"Hello?"

"This is Detective Roberts. I received a message that you may have some information concerning a one Jewel Sanchez. Is that correct?"

"That is more than correct, but I would feel more comfortable addressing this issue in person," the anonymous caller requested.

"Well, if you would like to meet me downtown at the precinct, I can take your statement there."

Just as the words left Roberts' lips, Marcus snatched open the passenger's side door and got inside.

"Now…," he started.

"Shhhhhh," Roberts said covering the phone, "Like I was saying if you want to come down to the station, your statement on Jewel Sanchez can be taken there on the record." Roberts wanted Marcus fully aware that he had every intent and purpose on keeping his end of the deal.

"I would rather keep my face out of the police department if that is at all possible."

"Wherever you are, I can come to you."

Marcus overheard the conversation and was eager to get Jewel out of the way for good. Even though he couldn't get in touch with Diamond, he knew that the only place she could be was at her mom's.

"Tell him to meet us here. Tell him to meet us here," he whispered.

"Can you meet me now?" Roberts reluctantly asked. He knew it wasn't safe to meet up outside of the station, but with Marcus' foot on his neck, he had no other choice.

"Where?"

"Between 46th St. and 12th Ave."

"I can be there in ten minutes."

"See you then. What's your name by the way?"

"I go by Robbie." *Click.*

Roberts hung up the phone hoping the conversation was enough to appease Marcus. "We have a lead on Jewel. A guy by the name of Robbie stated that he can connect him to the murder of one of his crew members Brandon Edwards. If we can connect him to the murder in any way or better yet, find the body, Jewel will be going away for a very long time."

"Listen, Allyn, I don't care what you have to do as long as what you're being paid to do is done. Diamond is refusing to speak to me all behind this degenerate. I just want him gone," Marcus said slamming his fists into the dash board.

$$$$$

Pop and Sacario sat across the street from the parking lot Roberts waited in. Pop's curiosity wouldn't allow him to not know who was following them and why, so he watched as Roberts conversed with an unknown white man. The sight of the crooked cop sent chills up his spine as thoughts of his fallen cousin filled his mind. He felt like he was staring at the devil himself, but that didn't stop him from wanting to put a bullet in his head.

"Yo, who is that?" Sacario asked as he noticed Pop's fixation on Roberts.

"Detective Allyn Roberts. He's as dirty as they come. I should have known that he was behind all this surveillance bullshit. He has a fascination with getting rid of niggas even if that means they wind up dead."

"What you mean?"

"He killed my cousin like five years ago right in front of me just because my nigga was a young black male not dependent on anybody for anything. That's why he has a hard on for Jewel. If you shine too hard, you are definitely on his radar."

"Damn, that's fucked up," Sacario said completely aware of the double standards that existed within the legal system. He had encountered crooked cops more times than he could count. Soon he just believed they came along with the game.

$$$$$

"Marcus, calm down. I'm a man of my word," Roberts said trying to reassure his donator.

"I hope so, Allyn. I wouldn't want my father to get wind that you are incompetent at what you do. $100,000 is a lot of money for somebody like you."

"Is that a threat?"

"No, Allyn, it's a promise. If you can't deliver then I will find somebody who can." Roberts was annoyed by Marcus' bratty attitude, but his hands were tied.

"Like I told your father, and like I told you, I was hired to do my job for a reason, so please just let me do it."

Marcus reached into his pocket and pulled out a small black box. "Do you know what this is?"

"A ring?" From the size of it, Roberts could only assume.

"Exactly." Marcus slowly opened the box exposing a fifteen carat flawless diamond ring. "This is my future."

"I'm really happy for you, Marcus, but I fail to see what this has to do with me."

"Everything. This has everything to do with you. I want Diamond, but with Jewel in the way, I know that she'll never be able to fully let go. I don't like to be told no, Allyn, but with this right here, she'll have no choice but to be mine again. One thing I've learned is that everyone can be bought. Everyone has a price," he said closing the ring box. He knew that Diamond was used to the best, but he believed that he could show her better. Her rejection only fueled his obsession and lust for her. From the day he was born, he had everything happily handed to him, and Diamond would be no different.

Suddenly there was a light tap on Roberts' side window. Roberts barely rolled it down curious to know who the strange man was.

Counterfeit *Dreams 3*

"Can I help you son?"

"Are you Roberts?" Robbie asked.

"Yeah, who's asking?" Roberts asked rolling down the window a little further.

Without giving a response, Robbie put his gun into the car and let his bullets ring inside. Blood splattered against the windshield as he put a hundred rounds into Roberts and Marcus. Marcus dropped the ring box to the floor. He struggled to breathe as blood quickly filled his lungs, and Roberts died after the first bullet hit him in the chest. They never had a chance. After emptying his clip, Robbie walked away as if nothing happened. The deserted area allowed him to disappear unnoticed back into civilization.

Sacario and Pop sat back in disbelief. Pop didn't move the car afraid he would draw attention to them, but he knew that they had to get out of there.

"Yo, what the fuck was that?"

Pop was at a loss for words as he watched Kisino's youngest goon Robbie disappear into the streets. He decided against wearing any sort of disguise hoping to make the murder as clean and quick as he could. Kisino gave him one job to do, so it had to be done. No question. Pop knew that this had nothing to do with Roberts and had everything to do with them. GMB was answering back. Kisino wouldn't be satisfied until he got rid of the M.A.C. Boys, but he had to be the one to do it. He wouldn't allow anyone to take that from him.

"They're coming for us, blood."

"Who?"

"GMB. Me and Jewel went to one of their traps, and that nigga was the one he left alive. He wanted him to go back and tell Kisino that we weren't backing down, and that he would have to kill us first. This is his message to us. There's nothing left standing in the way now. It's war."

"We gotta find Jewel."

Pop slowly pulled out of the parking lot as he heard sirens quickly approaching. He took one last look at Roberts slumped down in the front seat. He couldn't say that he wasn't happy. He knew that Roberts had crossed so many people and had done so many underhanded things that he definitely got what was coming to him. Pop just wished that he was the one who put a bullet through his chest.

Sasha Ravae

$$$$$

As Jewel and Joe continued to talk, Jewel was uncomfortable, but he knew that this was his opportunity to ask Joe all of the questions he held inside.

"So have you talked to my mom?" he finally asked. It had been so long, but it was something that was burning a hole inside of him. Even though he had lived most of his life without them, he still thought about his mother and father every day.

"No, not in a very long time. The last I heard after the divorce was that she moved to New York."

"Typical," Jewel mumbled. New York was one of his mother's favorite getaway spots. He wasn't surprised that she left without saying a word. Suddenly, Jewel's phone rang. He thanked God for the distraction. "I gotta take this."

"Go ahead. We have all the time in the world, Jewel."

"Hello?" he said walking out of Joe's office into the hallway.

"J-baby, how you doing, man?" Kisino sang into the phone, "I have some really good news for you, boy."

"And what's that?"

"You know that pesky police problem you were having?"

"How'd you know about that?"

"Never mind that, boy, but just know Uncle Kisino knows everything. I'm calling to tell you that you won't have to worry about Roberts or any other Sacramento police officer for that matter. I'm here to say that Roberts is no more."

"Kisino, blood, if you don't quit talking in fucking riddles."

"I got rid of Roberts for you. He's dead. You can thank me later."

Jewel didn't know how to respond. Roberts was beginning to be an inconvenience for him, but not that much.

"I see you're at a loss for words, so let me explain. Roberts wanted to link you to Brandon's murder because he was being paid off by Marcus Moore. You know him, right? The white boy fucking your baby mama? Anyway, even though you and I both know that Brandon is dead because of you, I couldn't have Roberts getting what's mine, now could I? If anybody is gonna put a bullet through you, it's gon' be me. Fair and square. Roberts was getting desperate because you're

Counterfeit *Dreams 3*

always so smart, Jewel, you slick bastard you, so it may have come down to that. I am happy to say that Roberts won't be bothering you no more. Marcus either, but that was just a lucky bonus. Now there's nothing standing in between me and you. No more excuses. Get ready, Jewel," Kisino said hanging up.

$$$$$

Pop zigzagged through traffic as he drove aimlessly. He seen how easy it was for Robbie to take out Roberts, and he knew they would be next. The M.A.C. Boys had been so successful because Golden wanted it to be based on the group's integrity, but GMB had no cares in the world. They were reckless, and their recklessness is what kept them on top. They shot first and asked questions never because Kisino felt like reasoning was beneath him. He would push his way to the top, and push he did.

"This shit is getting outta hand," Sacario said pulling out his phone to call K-2.

The phone rang and rang, but before it went to the voicemail, K-2 answered.

"What it is, bruh?"

"Where you at?"

"Gabby's house. Why, what's up?"

"Ay, you seen Jewel? He's not answering his phone."

"Yeah, he's over here too. What's up though?" he asked sensing the urgency in Sacario's voice.

"I'll talk to you when I see you. Put Jewel on the phone."

"Alright, hold on." K-2 got up from the bed he and Gabrielle shared and put back on his shirt before leaving the room. He walked up the stairs to Joe's study when he ran into Jewel.

"Ay, is your phone off? Sacario said he's been trying to hit you."

"Naw, is that him?" Jewel asked motioning toward K-2's phone.

"Yeah."

"Hello?"

"Ay, nigga, we got a problem," Sacario began.

"Listen, I know already. Meet me at the office in twenty minutes. We'll figure this shit out then."

"Yep," Sacario said hanging up the phone.

"Grab your shit. We gotta go," Jewel said to K-2.

"Will one of you niggas tell me what's going on?" K-2 asked feeling left out.

"We gotta go," Jewel said walking back into Joe's office.

"Is everything alright, son?" he asked noticing the look on Jewel's face.

"Yeah, but something came up. I know that you said that Jailen could come over for a few days, and I really appreciate it, but do you think Reagan can stay too? I know that it's a lot to ask, but right now, I would feel better if she was here with you guys. At least I would know she's safe."

"Of course, Jewel. That is no problem at all. Can I help with anything else?"

"No, but I'ma have Reagan call you when they're on their way, okay?"

"Yeah, sure," Joe said nervous by Jewel's sudden departure, "Please be careful, son."

Jewel looked at Joe and didn't know what came over him. He grabbed Joe and tightly wrapped his arms around his father. He didn't know if that would be the last time seeing him, so he finally let his guard down.

"I love you, Jewel. Please know that. I'm begging for your forgiveness. I know I messed up, but God brought you back to me for a reason," he said kissing Jewel on the cheek.

"I love you too," he struggled to say. The moment was hard for him to process, but the words felt good to say. "Thank you again." Jewel broke the foreign embrace and headed down the stairs. K-2 was already by the door with Gabrielle begging him to stay.

"You ready?" he asked.

"Yeah."

"Keith, why do you have to go? You just got here," Gabrielle whined, "Jewel, can't you just go do what you need to do by yourself?"

"Naw, Gabrielle, honestly I can't. I'll have him back though," he said walking out of the door.

"Baby, don't worry, I'll be back. Love you."

"I love you too."

Counterfeit *Dreams 3*

"Jewel, it was really nice to meet you," Isabella said over Gabrielle's shoulder, "I hope we see you around here more often."

Jewel just smiled.

"See that went well," K-2 joked as they walked to their cars.

"Nigga, let's go."

$$$$$

Diamond sat on her mother's couch with her phone to her ear. She couldn't move. The police officer tried to explain that her phone number was the last number Marcus dialed before he was murdered.

"Murdered? Murdered?"

Even though she wanted to be done with Marcus, she lied to her mother about changing her phone number. She had to have the will power to stay away from him, but that didn't stop her from wanting to hear him beg for her. Diamond just wanted to be wanted, and he pretended so well. It had only been a few days since they last spoke, but each day she felt a little stronger. It was hard as the drugs slowly left her body, but she kept the image of getting her family back in her mind. She needed her son, not the drugs, or even Marcus, and she soon realized that Marcus used the drugs as a leash. It was a way for him to control her, but she refused to be controlled any longer. She finally set herself free from the prison she willingly created.

"I don't know why he was calling me," she said finally speaking up, "We haven't talked for like a week, but I have no idea who would do something like this to him."

"It appears that Mr. Moore had a cell phone, an engagement ring, and a wad of cash on his person at the time of the shooting, but nothing was taken from him or the other victim."

"Ring?" She was convinced that Marcus didn't have it all. "Well, it wasn't mine."

"Thank you, Mrs. White. Please contact us if you can think of anything that could help."

"I will."

Diamond knew that she should have felt differently about Marcus' passing, but something inside her was secretly relieved. She was finally free. The bind that the drugs had on her was a direct result of him. No Marcus, no temptation. Diamond quickly said a quiet prayer for him and his family. It was a terrible tragedy, but she had other things to focus on. She finally felt strong enough to go and fight to get her family back.

"Diamond, who was that? Is everything okay?" Paula asked coming out of the kitchen. The expressionless look she had on her face sent chills through her.

"Everything's fine, Mom. I was just on my way to Jewel's," she said slipping a fake smile onto her face.

"Jewel's? For what?" Paula was sick without her grandson, but Diamond's priorities had been in such disarray that she didn't want to confuse him, but Paula could honestly say that Diamond was looking like herself more and more each day. Whatever demon had a hold on her had finally let go. She just hoped it was for good this time.

"What do you mean for what? For my son, Mom. I know that after everything that happened, Jewel may not want to see me right now, but I am still Jailen's mother. We haven't gone to court. He doesn't have custody, so I have a right to see my son."

"Just be careful please. Use your head. I don't want you and Jewel fighting in front of my baby."

"I can be civil, Mother. I just want to talk. What can that hurt? Diamond asked as she walked out of the door.

$$$$$

Reagan sat on the couch watching TV and rubbing her belly. This became her daily routine as she had no energy whatsoever to do anything else. With Jewel being in and out, it was nice to have Jailen around to help her around the house.

"Jailen, are you almost done with your homework?" she yelled deciding not to get up.

"Almost," he yelled back.

"Okay, let me know when you're done, and we'll go get something to eat. I gotta get out of this house. I need some air," she said talking more to herself.

"Okay."

Reagan continued to flip through the channels, but nothing was on. She became irritated at the lack of choices when suddenly her phone rang.

Counterfeit *Dreams 3*

"Hey, baby," Jewel said calmly.

"Hey, what you doing?" she asked excited to hear his voice.

"Nothing, on my way to the office. How you feeling?"

"Like I'm about to fucking pop. Only five weeks left to go."

"That shit is going by hella fast."

"Not fast enough," Reagan said sucking her teeth, "It's like no matter what I do, I can't get comfortable. It's so irritating."

"I know, but it's almost over, baby."

"Yeah, yeah, yeah, so after you leave from there, you coming home?"

"Not quite. I got some shit to handle. That's why I called."

"What's going on?"

"I can't talk about it right now, but I need you to do me a favor."

"Jewel, when is all this shit gonna end? I'm sitting here fucking 8-months pregnant, home alone with your son, mind you, and you're just M.I.A."

"I know, Reagan, and truly, I apologize, but I need you to hold on a little longer."

"I'm trying, Jewel."

"Where's Jailen?"

"Doing his homework. I was about to take him to go get something to eat after he finished."

"Okay, that sounds cool, but I'ma need you guys to go to my dad's house."

"Your whose house?" Reagan asked confused. Along with many other things, Jewel was very secretive when it came to Joe, so she didn't know what prompted the change.

"Joe's house. He said that you guys could stay there a couple days. I can't explain it right now, but things aren't safe for me. Meaning that they might not be safe for you either, and I can't chance that."

"So we're in fucking witness protection or something?"

"Reagan, stop being dramatic. I need you to be serious. It'll only be for a few days. Just until I figure this shit out. Please do this for me, Rea."

"Okay, Jewel, whatever. We'll go."

"He's expecting you guys. I'll text you the address. Call me as soon as you get there, okay?"

"Yeah."

Sasha Ravae

"Love you."

"You too," Reagan said hanging up the phone. She was beyond irritated. She was tired of Jewel's actions adversely affecting her. She was getting ready to have a baby, but she felt more alone than ever.

"I'm done," Jailen said coming into the living room, "What we eating?"

"Whatever you want, J, but we have to make a pit stop after."

"Where we going?"

"To your grandfather's house."

$$$$$

Dash sat at Kisino's desk as he waited for his mentor to arrive. It had been a couple of days since he was released from the hospital. He didn't feel a hundred percent, but duty called. After Jewel shot him in the shoulder and side, Dash barely made it to the back of the house. Pain penetrated his entire body as he crawled to safety, but he remained fearful of what the unknown masked shooters would do if they found him still alive. He mourned for his potnahs Mark and Tone's deaths, but he was thankful for his own life. Once the police came, they found him unconscious, lying on the ground in the backyard. The paramedics rushed him to the hospital hoping to stop the bleeding that continued to saturate his clothes. The doctors did everything they could to help Dash, but he knew that with gunshot victims came police, and he didn't have the answers. Not willing to cooperate, he left the hospital against medical advice with his fresh gunshot wounds in tow. He had been through this before, so he knew the routine. When Dash got back home, he found out that Mark and Tone had both passed away at the scene, but the shooters let Robbie live. He was relieved by his potnah's seemingly good luck, but he didn't understand why the shooters had pin-pointed them. Someone had to pay.

Dash tried not to move as his clothes rubbed against his blood soaked gauze when Robbie, Kisino, and Blue came into the room.

"Boy, get up," Kisino said motioning for him to get out of his chair disregarding his battle wounds. Dash got up and slowly walked to another seat across the room. "Thank you," Kisino said waiting for him to be seated, "Now I can catch you up on things."

Counterfeit *Dreams 3*

"What the fuck is going on, Kisino? One minute I'm at the trap counting money and busting knocks, and then the next minute I'm having two bullets pulled out my fucking body."

"You're alive, right? That's all that matters."

"Man, fuck all that. Somebody better tell me something. Robbie, nigga, you were there. What the fuck happened?"

"Let me explain, Dash," Kisino interrupted, "You being shot was a warning for GMB of some sorts. Jewel Sanchez felt like he wanted to let his balls hang for the day, and unfortunately, you all were collateral damage."

"Collateral damage?"

"But don't worry. Robbie, being the dedicated soldier he is, took care of it."

"How?" Dash asked feeling like Kisino's explanation wasn't enough.

"It seems our M.A.C. friends were having some trouble with the police."

"And? What does that have to do with us?" he asked out of frustration.

"It has everything to do with us. If it's hot for the M.A.C. Boys, in turn it's gon' be hot for us too. Plus I don't want to have any reason standing in between me laying every single one of these niggas down. With Detective Roberts outs of the way, Jewel has no more distractions. He's fair game now thanks to Robbie."

Kisino looked at his constructed soldier in admiration. He appreciated his ruthlessness and obedience. In the beginning, he only wanted to settle a debt, but when Golden refused, he began to see their long-term friendship as irrelevant. He wanted Golden to see that he wasn't the only boss. Kisino had high hopes that Jewel would bow down in his presence, but just as Golden did, he rejected Kisino's offer of splitting the M.A.C. Boys in half, but at this point, he didn't care about the money or the power that came along with the M.A.C. Boys. He just wanted to make them all suffer. It was the only thing that could relieve his sadistic frustrations.

"So what now?"

"We wait."

$$$$$

Sasha Ravae

After making sure Jailen was full from the chicken they picked up, Reagan reluctantly made her way over to Joe's house. She followed the directions Jewel gave her and was surprised by how close Joe lived. She wondered why he didn't make his presence known sooner.

"Why do I have to go over here?" Jailen asked uneasy about spending time with his newfound grandfather.

"Because your dad wants you to get to know your grandpa Joe. He wants you to have a similar relationship with him that you have with your grandma. That's all."

"But I don't know Joe."

"It's okay. We'll get to know him together, okay? I'ma be right there, and if you feel funny about anything, you let me know."

Reagan was uncomfortable being a part of the Sanchez family reunion without Jewel being there, but she had no other choice. Ten minutes later, she pulled up in front of Joe's house. She admired its simplicity. It was very modest, but she could tell that a lot of money went into it.

"You ready, buddy?" she asked as she parked in the driveway.

"I guess," Jailen said grabbing his bag from off the back seat.

"It'll be fine. I promise," Reagan said putting on a fake smile. During the time that Jewel had been gone, she made it her mission to protect Jailen. Not because she wanted him to forget about Diamond, but because with Jewel and Diamond both barely being in the picture, she felt she owed it to him. She didn't know what suddenly made Jewel so comfortable around Joe to leave Jailen with him, but she figured, no matter the reason, it had to be for the best.

She got out of the car leaving her own bags in the trunk not feeling like carrying them into the house. She walked up to the front door that was softly illuminated by the light sitting above it and rang the doorbell. She was very excited to meet the man who helped create the love of her life, but she didn't know what to expect.

"Reagan?" Isabella asked opening the door with a smile across her face.

"Hi, yes, and you are?"

"Oh, I'm so sorry. I'm Joe's wife Isabella. It's very nice to meet you. Come in. Come in." Isabella's seemingly genuine warmth was refreshing to Reagan. "And this must be Jailen," she said extending her hand.

"Yes."

"You are so handsome," she said pinching his chubby, caramel cheek, "You look exactly like your father. You know that?" Jailen just smiled at the compliment. "Well you guys make yourselves at home. I'll go get Joe."

Reagan watched as Isabella disappeared upstairs. She was amazed at how beautiful she was. She was in her late forties, but Reagan thought she looked at least ten years younger, but more importantly, she appreciated her hospitality. Both she and Jewel had come from not the best of homes, so it was nice to see how the other half lived.

"You remember me?" Joe's voice boomed into the room as he entered.

"Yes, sir," Jailen said remembering him from the first time they met. He assumed he was just one of Jewel's friends. He had no idea that he was actually his grandfather.

"Sir? Am I that old? You can call me Joe," he said sitting down next to Jailen on the couch, "So how you been?"

"Okay, I guess."

Joe looked up at Isabella who was admiring the family pictured in her living room. It made her heart happy that things were finally turning around. She was thankful for the life Joe provided to her, Gabrielle, and her oldest daughter Raquel, but not once did she want him to sacrifice his own son to do so. Jailen was Joe's first and only grandchild, and Isabella thanked God for the blessing.

Gabrielle came into the room still upset about K-2 leaving, so she spent the rest of the day sulking. "Oh, sorry, I didn't know you had company."

"Company? No, Gabby, this is family. You remember Jewel's son Jailen, right?"

"Yes, of course, Dad," she said offended. It wasn't every day that she found out that she had a long lost brother. How could she forget his son?

"Jailen, this is your auntie Gabby. This is your dad's little sister."

"Hi," he said shyly. The reunion was beginning to become too much. Jailen just wished Jewel was there too.

"Hi, I'm Reagan," she said finally introducing herself. She was amazed at how cute Gabrielle was. She looked like a smaller, female version of Jewel. Reagan had to admit that Joe had some strong genes.

"I'm so sorry, Reagan," Joe said noticing his own neglect.

"Hi, Jailen, you like video games?" Gabrielle asked noticing his disinterested expression.

"Yes," he said with a little more enthusiasm.

"Let's go play. I just got the Xbox One and the PlayStation 4. You pick," she said hoping to connect with her newfound nephew.

"Oh, cool," Jailen said as he jumped off of the couch.

Gabrielle was always able to convince her parents to buy her the latest and greatest of everything out of her exaggerated necessity, but within a week's time, she would become bored, but at that moment, she knew all of her games and gadgets would be perfect for Jailen.

"Sorry about that," Joe said happy to see his family coming back together, "It's just that I never thought Jewel would agree to this given the circumstances."

"And what is it that Jewel actually agreed to?" Reagan asked out of curiosity.

"Jewel is in trouble. He's mixed in with the wrong people doing the wrong things, but he insists that he has some sort of obligation to this lifestyle of his."

Reagan knew that Jewel was constantly taking penitentiary chances, but it's the life he chose to live.

"I kind of understand all of that, but what I don't understand is what that has to do with me and Jailen."

"I asked Joe to ask Jewel if Jailen could come over here," Isabella admitted, "I know that Jewel's actions have dangerous consequences, and I just felt like he would be safer here with us."

"But he was with me, and with all due respect, he doesn't know either of you, so how do you figure that he would be better off here?"

"She didn't mean it like that," Joe interrupted, "It's just with you being pregnant and all, we figured that it would be easier if you had some help. We're not trying to overstep our boundaries. I just wanted to get the opportunity to get to know my grandson."

"And I can respect that," Reagan said, "But I don't know what that has to do with me."

"Jewel felt like you would be safe here too. We have plenty of room."

"I'm a grown woman. I can take care of myself."

"That may be, but Jewel is going through some things. I just wanted to help him in whatever way I could."

"Why now?"

"Excuse me?"

"I mean it's been over ten years and not once did you reach out to Jewel. When we spoke, and he was in jail, you refused to help, but now all of a sudden, you want to be dad of the year?"

"People change, Reagan. I admit to my mistakes, and I am willing to do anything within my power to make those wrongs right. I understand that I hurt Jewel, but my intention is to never put him through that again."

"I appreciate your efforts, and I know this means a lot to him being that he doesn't have any family other than the guys he hangs with and being that Jailen's mother has been gone the past few months, but I am more than capable of taking care of us despite Jewel's activities."

Reagan knew that she agreed to lay low at Joe's house, but she was having a baby, and the idea of her being at a stranger's house made her more uncomfortable than ever. She just wanted to be in her own bed.

"Reagan, believe me, we understand," Isabella chimed in, "But will it still be okay if Jailen stays with us for a few days?"

"If it's fine with Jewel, it's fine with me. I'm just glad he's getting to know the other side of his family," she said grabbing her purse from the couch.

"I know you probably have to go, but can you stay for dinner?" Isabella asked hoping Reagan would say yes.

She didn't want to come across as rude, so Reagan agreed. "Sure." She wanted to blame her erratic hormones, but her instinct to protect Jewel and Jailen became natural, and she wouldn't apologize for it.

Isabella was thrilled. She hurried into the kitchen to put the finishing touches on dinner. Throughout the years, Joe had whisked her across the world to many upscale, five-star restaurants, but to her, nothing compared to a home cooked meal. That's how she showed her love. Once dinner was done, Reagan spent the rest of the night getting to know Joe, Isabella, and Gabrielle. Her initial impression of them was wrong. They seemed to be very good people. Reagan felt bad that she had hated Joe with Jewel, but she was only going off of what he told her. Isabella filled the table with cioppino, a fish stew that Joe adored, garlic bread, salad, followed by a bottle of wine for her and Joe.

"The food is delicious, Isabella. Thank you," Reagan managed to say in between bites.

"It's my pleasure. I love to cook. I used to think about doing it professionally, but that was a long time ago."

"You definitely could."

Isabella was pleased by Reagan and Jailen's response. He was usually a picky eater, but even he was asking for seconds. After dinner, Isabella brought out a tiramisu she had made from scratch.

"I hope you guys made room," she said cutting the first slice.

"I am stuffed," Joe said rubbing his small pot belly, "but pass me a piece, love."

"I couldn't eat another bite, but thank you though. I should really get going," Reagan said looking at the clock.

"How about a piece to go?" Isabella asked not ready to stop playing hostess.

"Sure."

"What about you, Jailen?"

"Is that cake?"

"Sure is."

"Then yes, please," he said making room for the foreign dessert.

"We'll take it upstairs, Mom," Gabrielle said hoping to distract herself from K-2's absence.

"Okay, I'll bring it up to you guys," she said walking into the kitchen.

"Jailen, come here." Reagan pulled him aside before he flew back upstairs.

"Yes?"

"You okay?" She was concerned about leaving him in Joe and Isabella's unfamiliar hands.

"I was nervous at first, but I'm fine now. Gabby has so many games," he said oblivious to the real reason he was there.

"Are you gonna be okay if I go home for a while?"

"I thought you were staying here with me?"

Counterfeit *Dreams 3*

"I was, but the baby has me feeling a little sick, so I think it'll be better if I'm at home, but I need to make sure you're okay first."

"I'll be fine. Grandpa Joe and Ms. Izzy are nice. I like them," Jailen said simply.

"You sure?"

"Yep."

"Okay, I'll call your dad and let him know, but he'll probably call to check on you a little later, okay?"

"Okay."

"I love you."

"I know," Jailen giggled, "I love you too."

"Be good," Reagan said rubbing his cheek before he sprinted up the stairs to eat cake and resume his video game tournament with Gabrielle.

"He'll be fine," Joe said sensing the hesitation on her face. "Believe me. I have prayed for this day."

"I know," Reagan said wanting to reassure herself.

"Are you going to be okay home alone?"

"Yeah, I'll be fine. With the house empty, I'll be able to get some sleep. This baby is kicking my butt," she said rubbing her belly.

"How far along are you?" Isabella asked coming up from behind Joe handing Reagan her slice of tiramisu.

"Thank you," she said reaching for the small plastic bag, "But I'm 8-months."

"Do you know what it is yet?"

"Yep, it's a boy."

"Another Sanchez man in the family, huh?" Joe asked beaming with pride.

Reagan didn't have the heart to disclose the complexities of her and Jewel's relationship, so she just smiled.

"And are wedding bells in our future?" Isabella asked grabbing her hand admiring the diamond that sat on her left finger.

"Let's hope so. We haven't set an exact date yet, but we will. I love your son very much."

"I can tell," Joe said smiling, "Well, you get home safe. We don't want to keep you, but please, if you need anything at all, don't hesitate to ask. You have the number, right?"

"I do."

"Use it."

"I will, and thank you for everything," Reagan said walking out of the door.

"It was our pleasure," Isabella said, "We hope to see you soon." Without thinking, she gave Reagan a hug. She was drawn to her instantly. She admired the role that she played in Jailen's life even though he wasn't her biological son. Isabella regretted that she wasn't able to develop that same relationship with Jewel when he was growing up, but it was better late than never.

Reagan walked to her car with a sense of relief showering over her. She imagined Joe and Isabella to be monsters, but they seemed normal enough, which was a change for her. She could tell that Joe just wanted to appreciate the simple things in life. No drama, and she envied that. She was excited about the expansion of her family, and even though the baby wasn't Jewel's, she was happy to know that she was beginning to have a family to call her own. The disjointedness of their relationship is what banded them together. They both weren't perfect, but Reagan could only hope that Jewel would be as good of a father to her son as he was to his own. Ready to tell him that there had been a change in plans, Reagan decided to call him.

"Hello?" Jewel asked answering on the first ring, "Everything okay?

"Yeah, I just left Joe's. Where you at?"

"At my office, and what you mean you left? Where's Jailen?"

"He wanted to stay. I know that you wanted me to stay there too, but Jewel, I am a grown-ass woman. I don't need to be babysat. I stayed, and I talked to them for a few hours. I had dinner. Everything went good. They were surprisingly really nice. I think you had them all wrong."

"Let me worry about that, okay?" Jewel said not ready to discuss the future with his father.

"You know I wouldn't of just left Jailen. He was having fun, and I told him to call home if he needs anything. It's only for a few days, right?"

"Let's hope so."

"What does that mean?"

"That means that I'm trying to tie up these last few loose ends as fast as I can, but you know how this shit goes, Rea."

"I really don't, but that's neither here nor there."

"I'm trying my hardest, Reagan. Do you think I wanna be away from him? Away from you and my family? I don't, but I will do whatever I have to do to keep you guys safe."

"I know, Jewel, just please be careful."

"Ain't I always?"

"No, so again, just please be careful."

"I love you, fat mama."

"I love you too."

"Let me get off here, so I can call Jailen, but I'll hit you back when I know more, okay?"

"Okay."

"Bye."

When she pulled up to the house, she was mad that she didn't leave the lights on. With all of Jewel's sudden precautions, she was starting to make herself paranoid. Reagan hated the time she had to spend away from him, but she knew that it was common for the type of life he lived. She wished that he would have followed in his father's footsteps and just lived a normal life for once, but she knew for Jewel Sanchez that was out of the question. Nothing was normal or regular when it came to them. Their relationship had been up in the air from the moment they met, but she wouldn't have traded it for anything. She knew that eventually they would have the life she had always dreamt of. The house, the kids, the wedding, she would have it all. She had faith in Jewel.

When she walked into the house, it was pitch black. She locked the door behind her and went to turn the lights on when there was a knock at the door.

Who the fuck is that? she thought to herself. At that moment, she hoped she wouldn't regret not taking Joe up on his offer. When she went to the door and opened it, she couldn't believe her eyes. It was Diamond. Reagan was at a loss for words. It had been over six months since she had last seen her.

"Jewel's not here," she hurried to say. She couldn't afford the drama being pregnant. Protecting her baby was her only concern.

"Why are you still here?" Diamond asked trying to mask the hurt in her voice. She had been calling Jewel for hours, but each time, he redirected her call to voicemail.

Sasha Ravae

"I live here," Reagan said simply, "And like I said Jewel's not here." She was not up for one of Diamond's soap-operaesque episodes. Even though she had taken an active role in Jailen's life, she didn't want to be involved with Diamond and Jewel's situation. That was for him to handle.

"You live here," Diamond mocked as she pushed the door against Reagan and brushed past her, "Where's my son?" She wanted to believe that there was still hope for her and Jewel, but with Reagan still around, she knew where his heart was even if she couldn't admit it.

"He's not here."

"Well, where is he?" Diamond asked as she surveyed her old home. Nothing had changed, but she felt like she was looking at everything for the first time again. It was colder than she remembered. The warmth and love that used to fill the house dissipated. Jewel had a new family now. A family that once belonged to her.

"Diamond, let's not do this, okay? These are questions that you need to ask Jewel, your child's father. Your problem is not with me."

"No, bitch, my problem is with you. You think you can come back and guilt Jewel, my son's father," Diamond emphasized, "into helping you raise that baby, and I'm not supposed to say shit? Fuck all that. Jewel will always be mine. I messed up, yes, but we have a son together. We have a family. You're just temporary. Thanks for keeping my spot warm for me, sweet heart."

Being that I've been mommy to your son for the past six months, you would think a bitch would have enough manners to say thank you. I guess not though."

"You will never be mommy, bitch. Is that what you thought? My son knows exactly who his mother is. Don't ever get it twisted. Jailen knows you're only temporary too."

"Does he?" Reagan asked flashing her engagement ring in Diamond's face.

Diamond stared at the stone in disbelief. Jewel and she used to joke around about them getting married, but he never took that extra step. She would have loved to solidify their family, but here he was wifing someone who was pregnant by another man. She didn't understand why she wasn't enough for him.

102

Counterfeit *Dreams 3*

"And what's that supposed to mean?" Diamond asked sucking her teeth.

"Did all those drugs fry your brain, bitch? It means that me and Jewel will soon be husband and wife. I win."

Chapter 6

Veronica sat at her desk staring at the phone that sat next to her. After Roberts was killed, word spread fast. She attempted to rush over to the scene, but her captain insisted that she stay at that precinct until further notice. He knew that she was the closest person to Roberts, and he couldn't let her emotions jeopardize their investigation. Veronica couldn't help but wonder if she had something to do with Roberts' death. She insisted he speak with the informant, but she knew that if he did, he would have come back to the station. Something wasn't right.

Ring. Ring. Ring. Ring.

The sound of Veronica's phone snapped her out of her guilt-filled trance.

"Matthews," she slowly spoke into the phone.

"Hey, Veronica, Roberts didn't make it. DOA."

"Any witnesses?" she asked as her breath escaped her.

"Not yet, but we're still casing the area. I just wanted to give you an update. I know it's hard losing a partner especially like this."

"We have to catch who did this, Williams."

"We will. I'll let you know when we have more. Go home and get some rest."

Veronica hung up the phone in shock. She wondered how someone was able to kill Roberts like a dog in broad day light without there being any witnesses. Even though her captain was against it, she was determined to catch whomever killed Roberts herself.

"Headed home, V?" an off-duty police officer asked as she grabbed her coat and left to pursue her mission.

"Yeah, I just need to get some rest."

"Take it easy. They'll find the bastard who did this."

$$$$$

Asaya sat across from Kisino with disgust in her eyes. She knew that Jewel had something to do with Brandon's disappearance, but he failed to lift a finger.

"What can I do for you, Asaya?" he asked as he lit the cigar that hung in his mouth. He kicked his feet up on his desk as he waited for her to speak.

Counterfeit *Dreams 3*

"I want to call off the hit."

"On who?" Kisino asked disinterested by her presence.

"On Jewel," she screamed, "It has been months since my cousin has been missing. You and I both know he's dead, and you and I both know who's to blame."

"Well why would you want the hit called off if you are well aware that Jewel is responsible?"

"Because he's having a baby. Well, he's not. Brandon's ex-girlfriend is."

"Okay? I fail to see what this has to do with me, mami. I am a very busy man, so I would appreciate if you didn't waste my anymore of my time."

"Brandon's ex-girlfriend is pregnant with Brandon's baby, but now she's with Jewel. That baby is the last thing that I have left of my cousin. I have to protect him. That's what Brandon would want even if that means letting that son-of-a-bitch Jewel live."

"Very honorable of you, but that's a no can do. You don't call the shots here, Asaya," Kisino said slamming his fists down on the desk, "I do. You're just an overpriced prostitute with a grudge. Why would I give a fuck about what you want?"

"I'm the only reason why you were after Jewel in the first place."

"Wrong again, sweet heart. This shit here is bigger than you and your bi-po cousin. Jewel's death is about principles, so if you don't mind, please get the fuck out of here before I change my mind."

"On what?"

"On if your life is worth anything to me," Kisino spat.

In the beginning, he thought that he may be able to use Asaya's passion as an asset, but soon she became a liability. Her emotions annoyed him.

"Asaya, I suggest you stay along for the ride. You wanted Jewel dead, and that he will with or without your blessing. After the cop I just had killed, I'm on a bit of a high. Don't get added to the list.

"Cop?" she asked realizing that Kisino was taking things too far, "What cop?"

"A one Detective Roberts. He was also trying to connect Jewel to Brandon's murder amongst other things, but his reasons were selfish, so I had him taken care of. No one, and I mean no one will stand in the way of me watching Jewel's life drain from his veins. I see it as just another casualty of war."

Asaya wished that she had never involved Kisino in the first place, but she now realized that his motives preceded her. "So if you already had it in for Jewel, why me?"

"Because you were easy to manipulate. You let your emotions blind you, and you were ready to kill him at any moment, just like a dog. I don't like doing the dirty work sometimes. It gets messy, but you let your feelings get in the way of what is most important, and that's me. Once I get rid of all the F.A.G. Boys, I will be king of the city. Not even the police can stop me, so how could you? Now be a good girl and run along. I'll call you if I need anything from you," he said dismissing Asaya.

She grabbed her purse from off the floor and walked out without saying another word. She had to warn Reagan. If Kisino was set on killing Jewel, what would keep him from killing her and the baby too? She knew Reagan wasn't safe. She had to do whatever she had to do to protect Brandon's son. There was no other choice. As Asaya quickly walked to her car, her phone rang.

"Hey, baby, can I call you right back? It's really not a good time," she hurried to say.

"Where are you?" Veronica asked.

"I had some things to take care of. I'm not a prisoner, okay? I'll be home later."

"Don't snap at me, Asaya. I was just asking. I don't have time for this. Bye."

"Veronica, what's wrong?" she asked. She could tell that she had been crying.

"Roberts is dead."

"Roberts?" Asaya asked remembering the name.

"Detective Roberts, my partner. I swear you don't listen to anything I say. Why do I even talk to you?"

"What happened?"

"He was found murdered in his car earlier today. I asked him to follow-up on a lead I had about Jewel's connection to Brandon, but I don't even know if he followed-up with it before he was shot in the chest. Oh god, what if this is all my fault, Asaya? What if Jewel or somebody found out we were tracking them and investigating

Counterfeit *Dreams 3*

Brandon's murder? He's dead because of me," she said beginning to cry again, "This is all my fault. I'm so fucking selfish."

"This is not your fault, Veronica. How can you even say something like that? You're a good cop."

"Am I? I did all this for you, Asaya. You've been so broken over Brandon's disappearance. You've been using again, drinking. You promised me all this shit would end a long time ago, but it seems like the more obsessed you became with Jewel, the further you fell into darkness. I just wanted to save you. I thought that if I could lock up Jewel for good that would free you from your pain, but I sacrificed Roberts in the process. I sacrificed Roberts in hopes that we would be okay again. That you would stop hoeing and just come home. I just wanted all of this to be over."

Asaya and Veronica had been together on and off again for over five years. Asaya was a prostitute when she met Veronica, but she hid her lifestyle because she was working as a police officer. After almost a year of being together, Asaya couldn't hide her hoeish ways anymore. Veronica felt conflicted. She took an oath to uphold the law, but she was in love with someone who was set on breaking them. Not willing to jeopardize her career, Veronica gave Asaya an ultimatum. It was either her or the life, and Asaya chose the life, but after only a couple of weeks of being a part, Veronica decided that she couldn't be without Asaya, so she chose to look the other way as her girlfriend continually sold her body and soul for money. The idea of random men touching Asaya made her sick to her stomach, but it was something she had to accept along with the other women, drugs, and neglect if she wanted to keep Asaya in her life. Veronica wondered how she became so dependent on the love that she was incapable of giving her, but Asaya was her first, and she didn't think she could be without her no matter how much it hurt being with her.

"Veronica, I need you to listen to me, okay? Jewel had nothing to do with this. I know who killed Roberts, and it wasn't Jewel."

"Wait, what? Then who did it?"

"Baby, I can't talk right now. I have to go handle something, but I promise we'll figure this out together. I'm sorry for everything. I shouldn't have gotten you involved. I'll fix this, okay? I love you."

"I love you too."

"Meet me at home in an hour," Asaya said hanging up the phone.

Sasha Ravae

$$$$$

Jewel and K-2 walked into Jewel's office finding that Pop and Sacario were already there.

"What the fuck is going on?" K-2 demanded to know. Jewel refused to talk about anything until they were all together.

"That nigga Kisino is a wild boy," Sacario said sitting down, "He had his young homie shoot that cop like it was nothing. In broad daylight at that."

"What cop?" K-2 asked completely lost.

"Kisino sent one of his hitters to kill the detective that was following us around these past few days," Pop offered.

"Why would he do that? Ain't that gon' make shit hot as fuck though?" K-2 questioned, "That's the last thing we need."

"Not really if you think about it," Pop continued, "With all of Sacramento on the hunt for some cop killer, they're not gonna be concerned with a bunch of street niggas, feel me? Our black asses can wait."

"At this point, I don't even think he cares about the consequences. He's so set on destroying the M.A.C. Boys all behind some shit he had going on with Golden. This shit is getting old forreal," Jewel said, "I mean if we gon' bang, let's bang. If we trapping, we trapping, but all these mind games he's playing is on some other shit. I'm not made for this."

"So what now? What's our next move?" Sacario asked lighting a blunt he had tucked behind his ear to calm his nerves.

"The nigga called me and said that he killed Roberts to even the field. He didn't want anything standing in the way of him laying us down, so I figure we give him what he wants."

"And that is?" K-2 asked still trying to understand the situation,

"Chaos," Jewel said, "Obviously me trying to keep it on a business level has made me seem like a bitch or something because ever since me and Brandon fell out, mothafuckas have been trying my patience, so I guess it's time to flip the script and ride on this nigga. What do we have to lose? If we sit back and don't do nothing, he will continue to fuck with us. I'm not living like that, blood. I can't even go home cause I'm scared somebody's following a nigga, and I won't be bring that shit to my house. I say we just end this shit tonight. I'm really not above laying a nigga out. I'm a reptable, blood. Niggas can check my credentials," Jewel said feeling his anger fill his chest. He never knew how covered he was by Golden's shadow. He didn't want to be seen as his protégé anymore. He wanted to be his own man. He wanted to remind everyone why he was chosen, so he could bring back the M.A.C. Boys from the brinks of destruction and lead them into victory.

"I know where we can find him," Pop interjected.

"What you mean? Why you just saying something now?"

"I didn't know all this shit was about to happen. I really thought GMB would just fall off especially after KP being exed out," Pop said looking up at K-2. K-2 never broke eye contact. He stood by what he did. Killing KP is what saved Gabrielle, and he would do it again.

"GMB has various houses around the city that they move weight and money at, but it's not on the scale that Kisino wants to make it seem. He's a Houston nigga, so all of his people are still in Texas. After he dried up out there, niggas wasn't really fucking with him. They were getting money before he lost his connect, so they planned to still do the same without him. When Kisino came to Sac looking for Golden, GMB was just Kisino and that fat nigga Blue. They managed to scrounge up a few desperate hood-hopping niggas..."

"Like you?" K-2 asked with a smirk on his face.

"K-2, blood, shut up. My bad, bruh," Sacario said wanting to excuse his disrespect.

"Naw, it's good. We can talk about it. I don't have anything to hide," Pop said turning to K-2, "Yeah, like me, nigga. Confused, hungry, ruthless, lost individuals such as myself. Kisino got dough, don't get me wrong, but he was never on Golden's level, and that jealousy is what made him start to hate him on the under. He wanted what Golden had. That empire, so what better way than to take one that's already established and slap a GMB tag on it?"

"M.A.C. niggas ain't fucking with him."

"Exactly, but that's not what he thought. Kisino thought that he could flash a couple la las, and niggas would come running not knowing we were bred for this shit."

"Well, he had me fucked up then, and he has me completely fucked up now," Jewel said, "So if he's not at the trap, where is he?"

"He goes from pillar to post. He doesn't want anyone associating him with GMB until he's able to take over M.A.C. He's at a Super 8 in the North the last I heard."

"So how do we get in there?" Sacario asked.

"Shit, we walk right in," Pop suggested.

"Let's go," K-2 said starting to get amped up, "My trigger finger has been itching like a mothafucka." Even though he knew how he was living was wrong, he lived for the street life. He couldn't imagine doing anything else. He would protect what Golden had built, and what Jewel intended to keep building even if it was with his life. The four of them grabbed their stuff and headed downstairs. "Should we take separate cars?"

"Yeah, we might as well. Sacario, you ride with K-2, and I'll follow ya'll."

"Got it," Sacario said ashing the doobie that still remained.

As they were walking out, Pop pulled K-2 to the side. "Ay, let me holla at you right quick."

"I'll be right down," he said throwing Sacario the keys to his car, "Man, what's up?"

"Listen, Jewel means a lot to me. He's like a brother, and I know that I betrayed him and the M.A.C. Boys in the worst way possible, but I will do whatever it takes to make things right again."

"What the fuck does that have to do with me?"

"What you mean? You killed my fucking cousin right in front of me," Pop yelled.

"And? You had no problem watching Will and Golden lose their lives, so I figured what's one more? Now we even, nigga, plus I was protecting my bitch. You remember her, right?"

It took everything in Pop not to punch K-2 in his face for his constant disrespect, but for Jewel, he kept his composure. "That's my point," he said exhaling, "Mistakes were made. People died, but I can't point a finger when my hands are dirty as fuck, so before shit escalates, I just want to squash the shit, and if you make Gabrielle happy then I'm happy. I'm not gon' sit here and front like a nigga don't understand what he lost, but she's a good girl, and I respect that she moved on. She made that loud and clear, and she deserves that."

Counterfeit *Dreams 3*

"Good looking, my nigga," K-2 said not knowing what else to say. He didn't like Pop, and he didn't think he ever would, but out of respect for his clique, he accepted Pop's words.

$$$$$

Asaya drove from Kisino's mad that she had ever allowed herself to become involved with him in the first place. He never had Brandon's best interest at heart, but she did. Now more than ever, she had to warn Reagan and Jewel about Kisino. Both of their lives were in danger, and she feared that they didn't even know it. She knew that Veronica was expecting her to be home, but she had to warn Reagan and Jewel for the sake of the baby. She drove to their house hoping that their encounter would be better than last time. She parked her car along the street relieved to see Reagan's car parked in the driveway. Asaya had to do what was right for her family and put her pride aside. She took a deep breath as she exited the car, but as she inched closer to the door all she could hear was screaming. Asaya began to walk faster as the screams continued to get louder and louder. When she got to the door, she found that it was unlocked, so she rushed inside fearing that she was too late. When she opened the door, she saw Diamond down in between Reagan's opened legs as she sat on the stairs, and blood was everywhere. All Diamond could say was, "Call 9-1-1."

$$$$$

Jewel followed behind K-2 as they drove to the North toward Kisino's honeycomb hideout. He was surprised that he would even be in a motel, but after finding out GMB wasn't as legitimate as they made themselves out to be, everything started to make sense. They were desperate. Even though he flooded Sac with soldiers, Kisino tried to keep his face out of the streets. He promised them somewhat of a promise land. They just had to be patient. Being from out of town, he already drew attention to himself. He knew that the M.A.C. Boys had everything locked, but that was slowly changing. Soon he would be able to be front and center as he took full credit for all of Golden's accomplishments and the empire he had built from the ground up, but until that happened, he just let his goons speak for him. Jewel tried to pump himself up, but he was just ready for it all to end. He was tired. He had been in the midst of war many times, but each of those times, Brandon or Golden was always there by his side. At that moment, he felt alone, but he knew what he had to do. As Jewel was driving, his phone rang. When he answered, it was the last person he expected to hear from.

"Jewel, it's me." From her voice, he knew immediately who it was.

"Diamond, why the fuck do you have Reagan's phone? Where is she?"

"A better question is why do I have to call you from the next bitch's phone in order to talk to you?"

"Because we don't have shit to talk about apparently, and we're not talking about the next bitch, we're talking about my soon-to-be wife."

"I heard."

"So where is she?"

"She's having the baby," Diamond said with no excitement. When she and Reagan were arguing, Reagan felt like the wind had been knocked out of her. Diamond assumed it was just her way of avoiding the issue until her panties began to fill with blood. After seeing the blood seep to the floor, Diamond's nurse-like instinct kicked in, and she remembered why she wanted to be a nurse in the first place. She loved helping people, and even though she blamed Reagan for Jewel's lack of interest, her conscience wouldn't allow her to leave her alone by herself. She had to help her, but that didn't change the way Diamond saw her. She just remembered giving birth to Jailen alone, and she wouldn't have wished it on her worst enemy.

"I came by to talk to you since you've been ignoring all my calls. When I got there, Reagan out of nowhere she started bleeding real bad. When we got to the hospital, the doctors rushed her to the operating room. The doctors said there were complications and had to have a cesarean."

"A what?"

"A C-Section. From what it seemed like, she had a placental abruption. It's not that common, but it does happen."

"Can you speak English please?"

Counterfeit *Dreams 3*

"It means that the placenta, the thing that connects the baby to the uterine wall separated from the uterus, so that's why they had to operate. Her bleeding was out of control."

"Fuck. Where is she?"

"We're at Mercy General."

"Tell Reagan I'm on my way."

"Jewel, we need to talk."

"About what, Diamond?"

"Maybe our son for starters. You do remember him, don't you?"

"Do you?"

"Jewel, where the fuck is he? He wasn't with this bitch, and he's obviously not with you."

"Don't worry about it. What you can do though is tell my girl I'm on my way," he said hanging up. After he got off of the phone, he called Pop.

"Hello?"

"Ay, nigga, Reagan's having the baby."

"That's what's up, bruh. You going up there, right?"

"I need to, but we gotta handle this shit first. I'm not gon' be able to focus on anything else."

"Jewel, go be with Reagan. We got this. This ain't my first rodeo, boy. I'll hit you if anything goes down. We good though. Kisino isn't as put together as he fronts to be. The nigga been acting untouchable for too long."

"Good looking, bruh. Hit me if you need anything. Let Sacario and K-2 know what's up, and ya'll be safe."

After getting off the phone with Pop, Jewel made a U-turn and headed toward the hospital. His stomach was in knots. He didn't know if Reagan and the baby were okay or not, and the fact that Diamond was there didn't make it any better. As he drove, he thought about his own son, so he called Joe.

"Hey, son, everything okay?" he asked nervous, every time Jewel called. He didn't approve of his son's lifestyle because it mirrored so much of his own. He knew how money used to control him, but he had to accept that Jewel was his own man.

"Yeah, I was just checking on Jailen. He good?'

"Yeah, Gabby tired that little boy out. He's been sleep for the past hour or two."

"Okay, good."

"Why, what's going on?"

"Reagan is at the hospital. She's having the baby, but there were some complications. I'm on my way there now."

"Is she okay? She was just here."

"I don't know. Diamond called and said that she started bleeding real bad, so I'm hoping."

"Diamond?"

"Long story."

"Ok, son, well keep us posted, and let me know if you need anything."

"Thanks, Pops," Jewel said hanging up the phone. The words sounded foreign coming out of his mouth, but it felt good to know that things were changing for the better with him and Joe.

When Jewel arrived at the hospital, the parking lot was packed. Not having the time to wait, he found a loading zone and threw his car in park. When he ran into the hospital, he searched for any sign indicating where Labor and Delivery was, but he found nothing.

"Hi, um, excuse me," he said to one of the volunteers who sat off to the side of the main lobby, "Can you tell me where Labor and Delivery is?"

"Yes, of course, it's on the third floor. Would you like me to escort you up there?"

"Oh, no, thank you. I got it," he said bolting toward the elevator. Before the doors closed, he managed to slip right in. When the doors opened, he stepped out into the hallway, and the first person he saw was Diamond. He hadn't seen her since the night he was arrested at Marcus' house. Despite what they were going through, he had to admit that she looked good. She looked like herself again.

"You got here fast," she said with her arms folded across her chest. She wanted to be mad, but she melted at the sight of him.

"Where's Reagan?"

"She's still in surgery."

"I need to be with her," Jewel said trying to find a nurse.

"They only allow one person."

"Okay?"

"Brandon's cousin Asaya is in there with her."

"Asaya? What the fuck does she have to do with Reagan?"

Counterfeit *Dreams 3*

"I guess she wanted to see her cousin be born," Diamond said rolling her eyes, "Reagan will be fine. The doctor said he would keep me posted."

"Like you give a fuck," Jewel said laughing.

"I got her here, right? Despite the bullshit, I am a nurse, and tonight made me realize that again, so can we talk now please? Just five minutes?"

Against his better judgment, Jewel followed Diamond out into the hallway that led to a small garden outside. The cool air caressed his anxiety, but his heart was still racing a mile a minute.

"What, Diamond?"

"Can you sit down?" she asked patting the seat next to her on a bench.

"I'm good right here," Jewel said refusing to sit.

"How did we get here?" Diamond asked saddened by his sudden cold nature.

"You know exactly how we got here. This is what you wanted, remember?"

"Is it? Jewel, me and my son almost lost our lives behind the life you choose to live. All I wanted was for you to fight for me, fight for our family," Diamond said beginning to cry.

"And I tried."

"Did you really, Jewel? The whole time we were together, your heart was with Reagan."

He couldn't say otherwise. He was always in love with Reagan. He was just hurt. He didn't know at the time, but he was holding onto Diamond and their relationship to distract him from Reagan, but in the end, it didn't work.

"I'm sorry, okay? I was in love with Reagan way before you came back into my life, but my son means everything to me. I love you, I do, but I'm not in love with you how you want me to be, Diamond, but that shouldn't stop us from raising our son together." Jewel had to be honest.

Diamond was at a loss for words. The only thing she wanted was for her family to be back together, but obviously Jewel didn't feel the same.

"So you were never in love with me? All that shit you said was just a lie?"

Sasha Ravae

"I thought I was. I think I was more so in love with the idea of settling down, but it's not fair to you or Jailen if I know that my heart isn't with you."

"So that's why you didn't care that I was drowning with Marcus?" Diamond asked feeling like her cries for attention went deliberately unheard.

"I let you do you, lil mama. I only cared when your bullshit started to affect our son and your parenting skills."

"He wanted me," she yelled, "With Marcus, for once, I felt wanted. Now I know that it was for the wrong reasons, but at the same time, it felt good. I can't lie. I just wanted you to want to be with me as bad as I wanted to be with you, but you didn't. Marcus was able to numb my pain in more ways than one, and soon I craved that numbness. I didn't want to feel anything anymore. Being high all the time eliminated me having to feel rejected over and over again."

"Diamond, please stop."

"I'm being real. At any point, if you would have called me and told me to come home, I would have dropped it all and came running."

"You don't have to drop anything for me. You are free to do and see whomever you want. Don't let me stop you."

"Marcus is dead, Jewel," Diamond said staring at the ground.

"What?" Even though he was well aware of his sudden demise, he didn't want to further incriminate himself. He felt like the less he proved to know the better.

"He was found shot dead in an unmarked police car. I guess my number was the last number he called, so the police called to inform me and see if I knew anything, but I hadn't talked to Marcus in a couple of days. I have no idea what he was even doing there. They said he had an engagement ring on him when they found him," Diamond said hoping to provoke some kind of emotion from Jewel.

"Ya'll were getting married?" he asked mad at her lack of good judgment. He would have never allowed a man like Marcus to be around his son.

"No, but I guess he was thinking about it. If he would've asked me, I would've said no. He was bad for me, and I knew that, but I became lost in him. In the beginning, I loved how he made me feel, but now I realize I compromised my whole life for him, and he let me. I don't know when I became this weak-minded person who looked to him for everything. I should have kept my independence about myself, but the fast-paced life he lived was exciting at first. In the end, it ruined who I was, but I'm strong in my faith that after all I endured, it's just a matter of time before all the pieces of my life are picked up again. After breaking up with you, I guess I needed to go through all that I did. It's dangerous to put everything you have into somebody, and I've obviously done that more than once for almost the same reasons, but now I see love doesn't work like that."

"Diamond, you know that I want nothing but the best for you, right? You're the mother of my child. I would never want you to be hurt or out here looking crazy. You've always been strong. You've been a single mother for years, and you've always held shit down with no one's help, and that's what I respected about you. I would never want you to compromise yourself for me or the next nigga at that," Jewel said finally sitting down, "I need you to know that no matter what I'm always gonna love you, D. We can get past this. It's just gon' take some work." He wrapped his arm tightly around her shoulder, and for a moment, nothing was said. They just stared up at the night sky admiring the stars, and let the silence surround them. For the first time in a long time, Diamond was finally at peace.

"I love you too."

$$\$\$\$\$\$$

Because of Reagan's complications, Asaya was able to go in with her. She informed the nursing staff that she was the baby's aunt, and she insisted she stay by Reagan's side. Not having time to waste, she was able to stay with Reagan. While she was in and out of consciousness, the surgeon slit the bottom of her stomach open releasing the life that God had created. Within the blink of an eye, unfamiliar cries filled the room, and Asaya broke down at the sight of her cousin. He was the most beautiful thing she had ever seen. She knew that she had made the right decision. After the baby was born, Reagan's nurse asked Asaya to wait out in the waiting room while they stitched her up and cleaned the baby. She was so excited about the life she watched come into the world that she completely forgot about Veronica. She knew that she was supposed to be home hours ago, but seeing Brandon's son be born was more important. After taking off her light blue surgical gown and mask, she stepped out into the hallway to call home.

"Hello?" Veronica said answering on the first ring.

"Before you flip out, I need you to listen to me," Asaya began.

"No, fuck that. Bye, Asaya. I asked you for one thing, and that was too hard for you to do. It's what I expected though."

"Reagan had the baby."

"What?"

"After I got off the phone with you, I went to her house. I had to warn them, but when I got there, Reagan was having some complications, so I called the ambulance. I didn't mean to blow you off, baby. You have to see him. He looks exactly like Brandon." As the words left her lips, sadness filled her heart. She knew how excited and proud he would have been, but she had to remind herself that through his son, Brandon Edwards still lived.

"I'm really happy for you, Asaya. I know how important it is for you to be a part of the baby's life, and I don't want to sound insensitive, but I have other shit to deal with."

"I know, and that's why I want to help. Protecting Brandon's son is my job now. He wouldn't have wanted it any other way. I will do whatever is necessary. When Brandon disappeared, he left me this weird-ass message about how if he didn't come and see me, he was at Jewel's. He kept repeating Jewel's name over and over again. I knew that they weren't speaking, but me and Brandon were never supposed to meet that night, so the message made no sense. I went to his house hoping, praying that he came home, but he never did. When I was there, his phone rang, so I answered it, and it was this man named Kisino."

"Kisino what?"

"Brown. I think his last name is Brown, but anyway, he told me that him and Brandon had been in communication a lot after Jewel and the M.A.C. Boys turned their backs on him. He said that if Brandon was missing then Jewel was a hundred percent behind it. Letting my emotions get the best of me. I just wanted to know something, anything that made sense, and he seemed like he had the answers. I went back to work, but every day that passed, I couldn't stop thinking about Brandon. Every day that passed my hatred for Jewel grew more and more, and it finally came to a point that if it didn't end, I feared I would've lost my mind. I became obsessed."

"If what didn't end?" Veronica asked. Asaya was so secretive when it came to a lot of things, so this was the first time she had heard the story in detail. Asaya had to hide a lot of who she was and what she did that it was hard for her to open up.

"I wanted Jewel dead, but for my blood's sake, I needed to be the one to do it. Kisino assured me that he would hand Jewel over to me on a silver platter, but he never kept his word. After I realized that he does everything on his own time, I figured it would be easier to take matters into my own hands, and that's what I intended to do. I went to Jewel's house ready to put a bullet right in the middle of his head."

"Asaya, are you tryna go to jail? You've been there before. You do remember what it's like, don't you?" Veronica was always concerned with her irrational impulses. She lived in fear of her safety because Asaya acted first and dealt with the consequences later.

"At that moment, I didn't care. Brandon meant a lot to me. He did a lot for me. He was the only person that I felt never judged me because I sold my pussy for a living. He saw the potential I had, and he invested into me. I know that you don't agree with what I do, but if it wasn't for my cousin, I wouldn't be at the level I am right now. I probably would be walking the blade somewhere, but Brandon saw more in me. I mean I got bitches working for me now, and I'm really at point where I don't have to hoe anymore. I can just stack off the backs of these broads. That would have never happened without him. He's always had my back, and I'll always have his even in death."

"Obviously, you didn't kill Jewel, right? So what does this Kisino guy have to do with it?"

"After I went to Jewel's that's when I found out that Reagan was pregnant. I hated her for how she did Brandon because I knew how much he loved her. I assumed the baby was Jewel's, but when she told me it was Brandon's, how could I hurt her? I instantly went back to Kisino and told him that the hit was off. The hatred I held for Jewel was soon replaced with the love I felt for my unborn cousin. At that moment, I knew it was my job to protect him. I just wanted Kisino to forget all about Jewel, but he said he couldn't."

"Why not?"

Sasha Ravae

"Kisino planned to kill him with or without me. He wants the M.A.C. Boys, but Jewel isn't cooperating, and after he found out that Detective Roberts was investigating Jewel, he had him killed because Kisino couldn't risk Jewel going to jail. He has other plans for him."

"Asaya, are you sure about this?" Veronica asked.

"Yes, why would I lie to you? Kisino told me out of his own mouth that he had one of his boys go and kill Roberts in cold blood. He said he was getting in the way."

"I have to talk to Jewel," Veronica insisted. She knew that Roberts was grasping for straws. He couldn't pin anything on Jewel, and he was desperate, but instead of looking at him as a suspect, he served more purpose as a witness. Veronica knew that if she could get him to testify against Kisino, she would be able to lock him up for good.

"Well, being that Reagan just had the baby, I know that asshole is probably on his way up here."

"Should I come to the hospital?" Veronica asked not wanting to overstep her boundaries.

"I mean if you think it will help. I'm just ready to put this all behind me, and with Kisino out of the way, the safer my chichi will be."

"Okay, I'm leaving now."

$$$$$

As Diamond lay in Jewel's arms, he was comforted to know that she had come back to her senses. He never wanted to fight, or take Jailen away. He just wanted to raise their son together without being in a relationship. Not wanting to give Diamond the wrong idea, Jewel remembered his purpose of being there.

"I should probably check on Reagan," he said easing himself from up under her.

"Yeah, I guess so," she said intoxicated by his scent.

They both got up and walked back into the waiting room. Jewel sat down next to the surgery doors hoping to receive an update on Reagan. Fifteen minutes later, a nurse all gowned up and her face covered with a surgical mask came bursting through the doors.

"Family for Taylor."

Counterfeit *Dreams 3*

Jewel immediately jumped up with Diamond right by his side. The sight of the nurse being covered in blood sent chills down his spine. "I'm her fiancé," he said, "Is everything okay?" Diamond cringed at the word.

"Everything is fine. We managed to stop the bleeding long enough to deliver the baby via C-Section."

"Can I see her?" Jewel asked.

"Yes, just give us like five minutes. We're moving her and the baby to our overflow unit."

"Thank you," he said relieved that she was okay. He sat back down anxious to finally see the baby.

"So can we talk about our own son now?" Diamond asked snapping Jewel from his thoughts of the newest edition to his family.

"With Reagan being pregnant, my dad asked if Jailen could spend a few days with him and his wife." He deliberately left out the continuous danger he continued to put him and his family in.

"Dad? Excuse me? You have my son around a fucking stranger right now?" she asked getting mad.

"He's not a stranger," Jewel said insulted that she would even question his parenting choices.

"Last time I checked, you didn't have a father, remember? Now you're telling me that my son is alone with this man?"

"First off, I've had Jailen the entire time you've been gone, and he's perfectly fine. Give me some credit, Diamond."

"Sir, I can take you to Ms. Taylor's room now," a small Filipino nurse said interrupting.

"Look, I gotta go. I'll holla at you later, and we can talk about everything, okay?" Jewel wasn't comfortable bringing Jailen back around Diamond until he knew for sure that she was done with her new life, but he couldn't deny the fact that she was still Jailen's mother.

"Okay," she said turning to leave, but before she left, she grabbed Jewel around his neck and placed a kiss on his lips. She missed the taste of him. "I'm not giving up on our family, Jewel. I love you, and I know that deep down, you still love me too."

When Diamond turned to walk away, Jewel was at a loss for words. He was confused by her kiss. He definitely loved her. They had a son together, so she would always mean a lot to him, but he was in

121

love with Reagan. He wasn't confused about that anymore. He knew where his heart was. Trying to put Diamond's display of affections aside, he followed the nurse to Reagan's room.

"Let me know if you guys need anything, I'll be right out here," the nurse said returning to her station.

Jewel slowly opened the door to see Reagan asleep with the baby lying on her chest. She looked so peaceful. He tried to creep into the room to get a better look at the baby, but his movements woke her up before he could get to her.

"There you are," she said with a slight smile.

"I'm so sorry I wasn't at home. When Diamond called, I came up here as fast as I could, but by the time I got here, you were already in surgery. They weren't tryna let me in."

"It's okay. I know that you would have been here if you could, but tell Diamond I said thanks for everything. Despite the circumstances, she really helped me. I hope that one day we can at least be cordial, you know?"

"Yeah, I guess," Jewel said not wanting to talk about her, "How are you feeling though?"

"Better now. When they first delivered the baby, they wanted to take him to the nursery because of all the blood, I guess, but I wouldn't let them. When they finally gave him to me, I broke down. I've never cried so hard in my life. He's the most beautiful thing I've ever seen."

Jewel walked closer to Reagan and stared down at the baby. All he could see was dark brown hair. He was excited and nervous all at the same time. He knew that being raised by Golden that a man could be a father despite the child not being biologically his.

"Did it hurt?"

"Yeah, I mean it hurt at first, but when they gave him to me, I've never felt anything similar to the instant love I had for him. The feeling was so strong." Despite Brandon's past indiscretions, Reagan knew that she had made the right decision for the first time in her life by keeping her child. "You wanna hold him?" she asked watching Jewel's eyes fixate on the baby.

"Yeah," she said nervously.

"I want you to officially meet Chase," Reagan said handing over her bundle of joy.

Counterfeit *Dreams 3*

"Hey, man," Jewel said touching his hand. He immediately latched onto his finger. There was no denying that Brandon was the father. When Jewel looked down at the caramel-colored baby that was all he saw. He didn't know what his reaction was going to be when Reagan actually delivered given the circumstances, but he was ecstatic. At that moment, he saw all of the goodness of Brandon embodied in Chase, and he was happy to have that connection again. He missed Brandon, so this was his chance to do right.

"Chase Sanchez, huh?" Jewel asked as he fell in love with his newborn son, "I like that."

"Sanchez? Jewel, I'm giving him my last name." Reagan knew what type of man Brandon was, and she didn't want her son to have anything to do with him.

"Taylor? Reagan, how does that make sense? If we're not getting married then go for it, but if we are getting married, wouldn't it make sense for us all to have the same last name? I mean I am signing the birth certificate, right?"

Even though Jewel knew that eventually he would have to explain to Chase who Brandon really was, he had every intention of raising him as his own.

"Are you sure you really want to do that?"

"I wouldn't be here if I wasn't," he said looking Reagan in her eyes.

"Okay then. Chase Taylor Sanchez it is then."

"That's better," Jewel said as he kissed Chase on the forehead. He hated that he never got to experience Jailen's birth with Diamond, so being there for him was special.

As the hours passed, Jewel stayed up with the baby tending to his every need as Reagan slept. She wanted to stay up with them, but she didn't have the energy. She couldn't even keep her eyes open. A few minutes later, there was a knock on the door. He walked over to open it when Asaya walked right in.

"What are you doing here?" Jewel whispered not wanting to wake up Reagan or the baby.

"It's nice to see you again too, Jewel. Long time, huh?" Asaya tried to resist the urge to make a scene there in the hospital, but she wanted answers about Brandon.

"What's up?" he asked not in the mood for chit chat.

"Where's my cousin?" she asked unable to keep her emotions in check.

"I don't know what you're talking about."

"Jewel, I know that you know where Brandon is or what happened to him. That's my blood. You, at the very least, owe me a mothafucking explanation."

"I don't owe you shit," he said as his voice rose, "Now if that was it."

"Can we talk outside please?" Asaya asked not wanting the situation to escalate out of respect for the baby.

"Naw, whatever you have to say, you can say right here," he said not wanting to hear anymore of her dramatics.

Reagan woke up and noticed that Chase was getting fussy by the back and forth conversation. "Baby, it's okay," she said holding him close to her chest. She was comforted by his scent.

Wanting the conversation to be over as soon as possible, Jewel agreed. "I'll be right back, baby," he said closing the door behind him. As he stepped out into the hallway, he was surprised to see no one other than Veronica.

"Is this another set-up? Cause I don't know shit."

"Like I said that was my blood, Jewel. You owe me some answers."

"First off, like I said I don't owe you shit. Secondly, I don't know shit, so if you'll excuse me, my son was just born," he emphasized.

Veronica hurried to speak. "Jewel, I know that I'm the last person you wanna see right now, but I need your help."

"Why the fuck would I help you? Bitch, because of you, I had to spend six months in County for nothing."

"Can I just have five minutes please?"

"Speak."

"I understand the time you spent in jail, Jewel, and I take full responsibility for that, but I was just taking orders. Detective Allyn Roberts had you and your organization under investigation because he felt like you were a link between several major crimes that were committed throughout the city. That investigation was supposed to bring you to justice for killing Brandon Edwards. That was my goal, but Roberts had his own motives, and I believe that those motives got him murdered."

Counterfeit *Dreams 3*

"And what does that have to do with me? Better yet, why the fuck should I care?"

"Because Kisino wants you dead," Asaya interrupted, "He told me that he had Roberts killed because he wants to get to you. You and I both know what he did, and if you're not careful, he's gonna do it to you too."

"Jewel, if you agree to give a statement and maybe even later testify, we could have enough to arrest Kisino. You and Asaya's statements are the only things that will put him away for good. The way I see it, with Kisino off the streets, we'll all be safe."

Jewel wasn't a snitch, and as bad as he wanted Kisino dead for killing Golden, he didn't want any parts of Asaya and Veronica's plan.

"I wish I could help. I really do, but I don't know what you're talking about. I don't know a Kisino. I don't know what happened to Brandon, but even if I did, again, why the fuck would I help you?" he asked as he disappeared back into Reagan's room leaving Asaya and Veronica back where they had started.

Chapter 7

Pop, Sacario, and K-2 sat on Pop's car slipping black ski masks over their faces.

"You sure this is the only way we can get in?" Sacario asked surveying the hotel's parking lot.

"Yeah, I'm sure. Kisino rents out the top floor. The hotel manager gave him the plug on the rooms for a fee. Kisino moves weight from out of here from time to time, and gives dude $50,000 each month to look the other way. If we go in there asking for Kisino, they're gonna act like he's not there cause technically he's not supposed to be there, so I figure we mask up, run in there, go straight to the nigga's room, do what we need to do, and then head down through the emergency exit through the back stairwell."

"Sounds like a plan to me," K-2 said eagerly putting his .45 in his waist band.

"Naw, K, you stay here. If we gotta be in and out then I need you parked over there ready to go when we come out."

"That's some bullshit," he spat, but he walked around to the driver's side as Pop and Sacario got out of the car.

"Park right there," Sacario said pointing to the other side of the parking lot.

"I heard you, nigga," K-2 said driving off.

"How you even know he's here?"

"He's always here," Pop said, "Follow me."

He and Sacario crept to the side door. It was unlocked, so they walked right in. Pop didn't want to hurt anybody. He only had his eyes set on Kisino, but he wasn't above laying out whoever was in the way. Once inside, they hurried to the elevators. This was the only way up to the top floor. The quiet lobby allowed them to go unnoticed. Pop was not surprised that more people weren't around. When Kisino was conducted business, the hotel manager usually made everyone scarce. He couldn't afford his staff knowing about his illicit financial arrangement.

"Ay, there's gonna be more people here than I thought," Pop said as he watched the floor numbers continue to illuminate. They were almost to the top.

Counterfeit *Dreams 3*

"What that mean?" Sacario asked. Just as the words left his mouth, the elevator doors flew open revealing two arm guards who were standing in front of Kisino's room holding sawed-off shot guns. Before they could move, Pop pulled out his gun and shot them both in the head. The two burley men dropped to the floor with no hesitation.

He knew that Kisino was probably having his weekly meeting, but he didn't know how many would be in attendance. Before they could get inside, Dash and Robbie came out after hearing the seemingly close gunshots. Surprised by the masked intrusion, Robbie pulled out his gun and pointed it toward Pop, but before he let off a shot, Sacario hit him in the mouth with the shot gun he took from the dead doorman. Robbie fell to the ground as blood began to form a pool in his mouth. Dash fired one towards the elevator. Pop hit the floor not knowing where the bullet would land.

"Put your gun down, or I'll blow this nigga's head off right now," Sacario said pointing his gun at Robbie. Dash didn't want to chance it, so he complied.

"Where the fuck is Kisino?" Pop asked.

"He ain't here, breh," Dash said.

Sacario could hear shuffling inside the suite. "Who else is in there?"

"Nobody," Dash lied.

With Sacario's eyes on Dash, Robbie tried to reach for his gun that sat on the ground. Out of the corner of his eye, Sacario saw Robbie's hand move, so he quickly pulled the trigger. Blood and brains splattered against the snow white wall as Dash used the distraction to run back inside the room, but Pop chased after him. Once inside, Dash climbed down into a hole that sat on the floor. By the time Pop and Sacario got to the secret door that led to an unknown stairwell, he was nowhere in sight. The entire time they had all been in the hall, Kisino and Blue used that time to escape the attack. Dash shot a couple more bullets from the bottom of the secret door, but then he disappeared into the darkness just as Kisino and Blue had. He hated that he had to leave his fallen brother dead and alone, but he vowed that his blood was not spilled in vain. GMB was on the rise.

$$$$$

Sasha Ravae

Two Days Later...

It had been two days since Jewel was in the hospital with Reagan. He hadn't heard anything from either Pop or K-2, so he was beginning to worry, but being with Reagan and Chase made it a little easier.

"Okay, you guys ready?" a chipper nurse asked as she gathered Reagan's discharge paperwork.

"Just about," she said holding Chase against her chest, "Jewel, did you bring the car seat up here?"

"Got it," he said holding up the small animal-covered seat.

"Well, I guess we're ready then."

The nurse helped Reagan into the wheelchair she had waiting for her. She was anxious to get out of the hospital. All of her other experiences had been so negative that the smell of the building made her sick to her stomach. Chase slept soundly as she and Jewel made their way downstairs to the car. At that moment, she looked down at who she thought was going to be the biggest mistake of her life and praised God for her son's presence. She was in love. Once outside, Jewel hurried to get Reagan and the baby softly loaded into the car. He was happy to be going home with his family. All that was missing was Jailen.

"Hey, son, how's everything?" Joe asked with excitement in his voice.

"It's going. Me, Reagan, and the baby are on our way home from the hospital now. I was going to go home and get them situated and then I'll be on my way to get Jailen," Jewel said as he got into the car.

"Don't go out of your way, Jewel. I can bring him. Plus I definitely want to see my new grandson. What's his name?"

"Reagan named his Chase," Jewel said not wanting to reveal the truth about her baby not being his. He planned to raise him as his own, and he didn't want there to be any differences made between his two sons.

"Chase Sanchez. I like that. I'll give you guys sometime to settle in, and then we'll be on our way."

"Thanks again, Joe. I really appreciate this."

"It was my pleasure," he said hanging up the phone.

"Is everything okay?" Reagan asked as she continued to look back and check on Chase. Her nerves were on edge with every bump.

Counterfeit *Dreams 3*

"Yeah, Joe said he would bring Jailen home a little later."

"That's good. Now we can just go home and relax."

"I wish I could, babe, but..."

"Jewel, don't start. Please don't tell me you think that after popping this guy out only forty-eight hours ago, you call yourself leaving me home alone with two kids to take care of."

"What choice do I have, Rea? This is something that I have to do. I can't put you guys in danger. I refuse it."

"Jewel, why don't you just go to the police? I know that there must be something they can do. I think Asaya's girlfriend works for Sac PD. We can talk to her."

"That's not the life I live, Rea. It's not an option."

"So what? Either you're gonna kill this nigga, or God forbid, he kills you. Either way, it won't turn out good."

"That's the chance I have to take," Jewel said ending the conversation. He hated discussing work with Reagan. He knew that his life put her in danger enough, so the less she knew the better.

Twenty minutes later, he pulled up to his house. As he was parking in the driveway, he saw Pop, Sacario, and K-2 standing in front of the front door. The sight of them put his mind at ease.

"What are they doing here?" Reagan asked rolling her eyes.

"Let's see," Jewel said getting out of the car as he helped her inside.

"What's up with bruh?" Sacario asked as he helped them with their bags.

"Ya'll come inside," Jewel said as he grabbed Chase.

"So this must be the newest edition to the camp?" Pop asked, "Congratulations, Reagan." He grabbed her tightly unaware of the freshly placed stitches that lined her stomach.

"Thank you, Pop," she said as she winced in pain, "This is Chase."

"Ay, Jewel, can I holla at you?" Sacario asked needing to interrupt the moment.

"Yeah, ya'll go in the living room. Give me like five minutes."

Pop, Sacario, and K-2 headed into the living room as Jewel escorted Reagan into their guestroom.

"Now I know you probably want to be in our room, but I think that until you heal up a little more, you should stay down here still. I don't want you breaking your stitches trying to carry Chase up and down the stairs."

"I don't care about none of that. I just want to lay down."

"Do that. Let me know if you need anything. I'll be right out here."

"I love you, Jewel."

"I love you too, Rea."

"We need you here." She was always in fear of Jewel's life. He was so trusting, and that trust always seemed to get him hurt. She just didn't want it to happen again.

"I know. I want to be here, Reagan. Believe me I do. I just need a little more time, okay?" Jewel closed the door behind him as he left the guestroom and walked into the living room ready to hear the good news. "So what's up? I've been trying to call ya'll for like three days. What happened?"

"Pop led us right to Kisino. He was crammed into some Super 8 off Bannon. There weren't any people around, so we were able to make it to Kisino's floor unnoticed."

"And?"

"And the nigga must have been linking up with his team cause he had two security guards posted in front of the room door. We took them out, no problem, but then two of his young homies came out blasting. Kisino used them as a distraction. We lost him, blood."

"Fuck. Fuck. Fuck," Jewel yelled, "So what now?"

"This back-and-forth shit can't keep happening," Pop said, "We gotta think of something because time is running out."

"See, man, that's why you weak-ass niggas should have brought me in. I never miss," K-2 spat.

Just as the words left his mouth, Jewel's phone rang. With no energy left, he didn't look at the caller ID. He just answered it.

"Hello?"

"Sending your niggas to do your job, huh? I guess you are thinking like a boss. Listen, I don't have time for this nonsense, so I just need you to listen, young blood. You sent these niggas over here ill-prepared as usual. I have to admit it though. They were so close, but now the terms have changed. You obviously don't know how to lead your troops, Jewel, so why don't you just leave it to me? In exchange for your life and the lives of your family, not only do I want your shares in Sanchez & Associates, I want that black-ass nigga Pop. I understand that because of legal reasons, you were unable to make good on our original agreement, but I'm feeling generous, so I'm gonna give you another chance. Pop is a cancer in the M.A.C. Boys if you haven't noticed already. He has no loyalty to you, so why do you think he can be trusted now? What's keeping him from turning on you again? I'm doing us both a favor if you really think about it. Meet me off Stockton and Mack tomorrow night with that nigga in hand, and we'll call it even," Kisino said hanging up.

Jewel remained silent. He knew that Pop was a liability to the clique, but he refused to turn his back on him. He couldn't lose another brother.

"Who was that?" Pop asked noticing the change in Jewel's face.

"Kisino."

"What the fuck did he say?" K-2 asked.

"He said what he's been saying," Jewel said frustrated with the circumstances, "He wants Pop."

"What?" he asked.

"Before I went to jail, Kisino hit me and said that in exchange for you, he would fall back. He thinks I sent you over to GMB to spy or some shit, but I said fuck that, and I'm saying fuck that now."

"I say we hand him over," K-2 said simply.

"K, blood, come on."

"Not like that. I mean if Pop is the only way we can get in this nigga's presence then I say we take that opportunity. We can finally end this shit once and for all."

"We can't just use Pop as bait," Jewel interrupted, "I wouldn't do that to any of you. It's too risky."

"Maybe not," Pop said, "I mean a lot of this is my fault, and Kisino is right. Clique hopping can get you killed. I say we take him up on his offer. If you act like you're turning me over, his defenses may be down. This might be our last chance to make this right, Jewel."

"What if something goes wrong?" he asked not willing to take the risk.

"It won't. If me and you go in there, and we have Sacario and K-2 there too, I know we can take out Kisino and that big, greasy-ass nigga Blue with no problems. We have to do this, Jewel. I refuse to spend the rest of my life looking over my shoulder all the fucking time."

Sasha Ravae

Jewel was completely against the idea, but he knew Pop's heart was set on making things right again. "Okay then, we'll meet up with Kisino tomorrow night."

"I'm in there this time," K-2 chimed in, "You niggas obviously don't know how to put in work. Like I said, I never miss."

"Let's go," Sacario said pushing him toward the front door, "You good, J? You need anything?"

"Naw, I'm good."

"Alright, I'ma hit you in the morning."

"Ya'll be safe."

"Always, brotha," K-2 said getting into Sacario's car.

Before Pop walked out of the door, Jewel pulled him back inside. "Pop, are you sure about this? You don't have to do this. You do know that, right?"

"But I do, Jewel. A lot of the problems in our lives have been because of me. From the moment I met you, you have been nothing but good to me, and I've continued to fuck you over. First the shit with Brandon and now Kisino. I've made some mistakes in the past that I have to account for now. I can't keep running from my responsibilities. I put us here, so I'm gonna get us out and that's a promise. I know that you've always seen something in me that I never really saw in myself. That potential. I want to see it though. I owe you for everything, Jewel. I messed up, but this will be the last time. I promise you that."

Jewel knew that he had his mind made up, and nothing he could do or say would change that. If Pop was adamant about putting himself in Kisino's grasp then he would do whatever he could to get him out of it. He had no other choice.

"No matter what, we're brothers," Jewel said, "So whatever we have to do, we'll do it together. No man left behind."

"No man left behind," Pop repeated, "I'll hit you in the morning."

$$$$$

Asaya sat and stared at the picture that covered her screen. Reagan texted her a picture of Chase all bundled up after they left the hospital to thank her for all her help. He was breathtaking.

132

Counterfeit *Dreams 3*

"Are you sure you want to do this?" Veronica asked as she continued to tape small microphones down onto her chest.

"What other choice do I have? If Jewel is too much of a bitch to put Kisino away then I will have enough balls for the both of us."

"I changed my mind, Asaya. I don't want you to do this anymore. What if something goes wrong?"

"It won't. All I have to do is get Kisino to confess to killing Roberts again, and we'll have everything we need."

"At least let me call backup," Veronica begged.

"No way, Veronica. This nigga can smell the police. I'm just going to get his confession and then I'm leaving. I don't want you to be there either. Please trust me, okay?"

"I do trust you. It's him I don't trust. I just need you to be safe. I couldn't take it if something happened to you."

"Well good thing nothing is then, right? Once this is over, we can move on, but I have to know that Brandon's son is protected."

"I know. Okay, the wire is all set up. Whatever he says will be recorded. Once we get the confession on tape, he will never see the sun again. You know what they do to cop killers, right?"

We're about to see."

$$$$$

Reagan lay in bed trying to force herself to sleep. She was exhausted, but all she could do was stare at Chase. He looked so peaceful as he slept. She traced his face as her finger glided across his soft skin. She couldn't deny the similarities between Brandon and the baby, but they were something she tried her hardest to overlook. She wanted to see Chase as he was intended and not as a reminder of her past. She laid her head down next to his as she let the sound of his innocent breath soothe her. Just as sleep approached, the doorbell rang. Reagan quickly tried to get up before the sound woke up Chase. She fought through the pain with each step she took. When she opened the door, Jailen ran inside.

"Is he here yet? Is the baby here yet?" he asked with excitement.

"Shhhhh," Reagan hurried to say, "Yes, Jailen. He's sleeping right now though, so you have to be quiet."

"Can I see him?"

"Of course, but go wash your hands first."

As soon as Jailen ran to the bathroom, Joe, Isabella, and Gabrielle each filed inside.

"Hi, Reagan, how are you feeling?" he asked setting Jailen's bags down by the door.

"I'm okay. Just a little sore. Thank you so much for bringing him home. How was he?"

"Perfect," Isabella said, "We've had so much fun these past few days. Joe and I can't thank you guys enough."

"No problem. It's good for Jailen to be around his family, you know?"

"That's exactly how we feel."

"Can we see the baby?" Gabrielle asked eager to see her newest nephew.

"Sure. You guys can have a seat in the living room. You need anything? Water? Juice?"

"No, thank you though. I think we're fine."

"Okay, I'll be right back."

Jailen eagerly followed Reagan into the guestroom where Chase was still sleeping.

"Come here," she said patting the bed. She picked up the baby and gently placed him in his arms. "You're a big brother now."

Jailen looked down in amazement at the small, chubby baby. "Is he going to sleep in my room?"

"Probably not," Reagan laughed, "He's too small right now, and plus your dad and me made the nursery, so you both will have your own space."

Reagan felt blessed to have her family finally complete. She loved Jailen as her own, and she knew Jewel was going to be a wonderful father to Chase. She felt like things were too good to be true, but she loved the feeling.

"Let's go show your grandpa and grandma the baby. You ready?"

"Yep," Jailen said handing Chase back to Reagan.

When they walked into the living room, they ran into Jewel.

"Where you coming from?" Reagan questioned. She didn't even know he had left.

"I had to run out real quick, but I tried to get back before Jailen got home. How you doing, man?" he asked pulling Jailen to him.

Counterfeit *Dreams 3*

"Good," he said as he embraced his dad.

"Joe's here," Reagan said heading into the living room.

When they all walked in, Joe and Isabella stood up immediately, but Gabrielle stayed seated with her phone glued to her ear.

"This is my Chase," Reagan said handing the baby to Joe.

"Oh my goodness, Reagan, he is a doll," Isabella said as she carefully took the baby from Joe.

"Thank you."

"Son, you guys did good." Joe was amazed at how things were turning around. Only a few months ago, he wasn't in Jewel's life, and now he had the chance to be a father again and a grandfather to two beautiful boys.

"Gabrielle, get off that darn phone please and come see your nephew. Can you spare five minutes?" Isabella snapped.

"Babe, let me call you back," she said into the phone. She got up and began to admire Chase along with everyone else. "I'm sorry. That was Keith."

"You can call him back later. Family is more important."

"I know," she said looking at Jewel, Reagan, and the kids. "Jewel, can I talk to you for a minute?"

"Yeah, sure, let's go outside." He wanted to learn how to be a brother to Gabrielle, but he didn't want her to get hurt again.

When they got outside, he sat down on the stairs and patted the ground next to him. Gabrielle quickly followed his lead.

"So what's up?"

"Keith called and cancelled our plans tonight," she whined.

"Okay?"

"He said that ya'll have business to take care of."

"If that's what he said then that's what he said."

"Look, I don't expect you to tell me what's going on, but just promise me that you guys will be safe."

"I really try to be, Gabrielle," Jewel said looking down at the ground.

"I really love Keith. More than I have ever loved anyone else even Pop, which is hard for me to admit. I don't agree with what ya'll do, but I know that Keith is gonna do him regardless, so all I can do is pray that he makes it home."

"Don't be so dramatic."

Sasha Ravae

"It's not about dramatics, Jewel. This is real life. You should know that. I mean what is all this for? You put your life on the line every day for what? Money? From the looks of things, you're not hurting, my nigga."

"Honestly, at this point, it's not even about that."

"Then what is it about? I spent so much of my time trying to figure out why Pop did the things he did, and I eventually kind of understood why. I mean for Pop, he came from nothing, so when the M.A.C. Boys put him on, he finally had a little money in his pocket. You guys gave him a sense of security, but he lost himself in the process. Is that what you want, Jewel?"

"No disrespect, but I'm not gonna get lectured by no little-ass girl."

"All I'm saying is what's after this? You have two kids now. I know that in the past Dad was a horrible parent, but I know he's not that person anymore. I've seen the kind of man he is my whole life. I see now that you got into this shit because you've been trying to run away from the person you used to be. It's time to stop running."

"I'm not that person anymore, Gabrielle. That's what people fail to realize. This isn't a fucking act. I am who I am today because of the choices I made, and I understand now that Joe made some mistakes and by holding that hate in my heart, it only affects me. By no means am I about to give this nigga a 'Dad of the Year' award, but we're working on things. In all reality, I have an obligation to my niggas. They ride for me, and I ride for them. They've been my family."

"Those kids are your family, Jewel. What's gonna happen to them if you get killed or end up going back to jail? You're basically doing the same thing Dad did. Leaving them with no father. I know you're smarter than this, Jewel."

"Why you preaching to me? Tell this shit to K-2."

"Don't you think I have?"

Jewel was uncomfortable with the conversation, but he couldn't deny that what Gabrielle was saying was true. With Brandon not around, Chase was going to grow up with Jewel as his dad. He knew what it was like to not have a father, and he didn't want the same for his kids.

Counterfeit *Dreams 3*

Jewel and Gabrielle sat on the stairs and let the quietness of the night surround them. A few minutes later, a car pulled up in the driveway.

"Who's that?" she asked.

"Jailen's mom," Jewel said recognizing Diamond's car.

"Baby mama drama, huh?"

"We'll see I guess."

Diamond got out of the car looking better than she had in months. It was going to be a long road, but she was beginning to get her light back. She refound her purpose. It had been a few days since they had seen each other, and Jewel hoped that she had gotten the idea of them being together out of her head. He just wanted to be the best parents together for Jailen.

"Hi, Jewel," she said walking toward the front door, "You busy?"

"Naw, why, what's up?"

"I was praying that Jailen was here. I am literally dying to see my son, Jewel."

"Let me give you guys some privacy," Gabrielle said getting up.

"Hi, I don't think we've met," Diamond said extending her hand, "I'm Diamond. Jailen's mom."

"It's nice to meet you. I'm Gabby," Gabrielle said as she shook her hand, "Well let me get in here. I'll see you inside, Jewel."

Diamond waited until she was in the house before she spoke. "Gabby? Isn't she a little young for you, Jewel?" she asked unable to mask her jealousy.

"Chill. That's my sister, okay? My Pops and his wife came to see the baby if that's alright."

"What you do is your business. I don't want to argue with you. I just want to see my son."

"Fine," he said getting up, "But before you do, I need you to promise me that this in-and-out shit is done. It's not fair to Jailen, Diamond."

"I know I fucked up. I took you and our family for granted, but that is all behind me now. I can't change what happened in the past. I can just do better moving forward."

"As long as we're both on the same page, I'm good, D."

Diamond followed Jewel into the house as he opened the door.

Sasha Ravae

"Jailen, come here for a second. I have a surprise for you," he yelled. Diamond stood behind him in anticipation. It had been months since she had seen her son. She missed him more than he would ever know.

Jailen came running into the foyer when he locked eyes with Diamond. "Mom," he yelled as he ran toward her.

"Hi, baby, how are you?" she asked bending down to accept his long awaited embrace.

"Where have you been?"

"Never mind that," she said placing pink kisses all over his face.

"Jewel, I think we're gonna hit the road," Joe said coming out of the living room.

"Thanks again for bringing Jailen home."

"It was our pleasure, Jewel. Isabella and I can't thank you enough. I hope to see more of you guys soon."

"We'll work something out."

"Hi, I'm Diamond," she said extending her hand to Joe. She couldn't deny that he was Jewel's father. Their likeness was indisputable.

"You must be Jailen's mom. It's very nice to meet you."

"You too. Sorry you have to go so soon," she said.

Reagan walked out from the living room surprised to see Diamond standing there. She hated that Jailen was put in the middle of her and Jewel's drama, but she knew he needed his mother. She looked at Jailen as he own, but there would never be a replacement for Diamond.

"Hi, Diamond," Reagan said smiling happy to see the reunion take place before her eyes.

"Hey, Reagan, how are you feeling?"

"Better, thank God. Thank you again for all your help. I don't know what would've happened if you weren't here."

"Please don't thank me. My nursing instinct just kind of kicked in."

"Well, whatever it was thank you. Jewel, I'm gonna go lay Chase down. He's getting kind of fussy."

"He's probably hungry," he suggested.

"Yeah, you're right," Reagan said walking over to Joe and Isabella for one last hug, "Bye, guys. Thank you so much for coming to see the baby."

138

Counterfeit *Dreams 3*

"It was our pleasure."

"We'll see you guys later," Joe said.

"Hey, Reagan, let me help you," Diamond said following her into the guestroom, "Come on, Jailen."

Joe, Isabella, and Gabrielle stood by the door as Jewel waited for them to finish their goodbyes.

"I'll give you guys a call later on in the week. Maybe we can set something up."

"Sounds like a plan," Joe said as he headed out the door holding onto Isabella's hand.

"Bye, brother." Gabrielle slowly walked over to Jewel and wrapped her arms around his waist. Her head fell against his stomach as she awkwardly held onto him.

"What this for?" he asked holding his hands up as Gabrielle continued to squeeze.

"I just want you to know that I love you. We all do. I know that we didn't meet on the best of terms, but you're my brother. Just remember what I said, okay?"

"I will," he said slowly wrapping his arms around Gabrielle, "I promise."

She hoped her words would change Jewel's mind, but she knew if he was anything like K-2 then that would be almost impossible to do.

"Everything okay?" Reagan asked walking out of the guest room.

"Yeah."

"Listen, I know that this might be weird of me to ask you…"

"What?"

"Jailen hasn't seen Diamond since she's been gone, right? I just think that maybe it would be nice if they got to spend some time together, you know?"

"I agree."

"So, I was thinking that since I'll be busy with Chase, maybe Diamond could stay for a few days?"

"Why would she do that?"

"I want Jailen to see that we can be one family, plus it's getting late. I know that Jailen is probably tired. I'm just trying to help."

"Did she ask you to stay?"

"No."

"I mean that's fine is she wants to wait until tomorrow to take Jailen with her to her mom's for a few days, but I'm not feeling having my fiancé and the mother of my son playing Brady Bunch and shit. I just don't want to confuse things."

"Confuse what?" Diamond asked walking out of the room.

"Nothing," Jewel said not wanting to discuss the situation in front of Jailen. "Ay, J, go get the guestroom upstairs ready for your mom. She's gonna spend the night, and then you guys are gonna go see grandma P in the morning."

"Are we really, Mom?" he asked with excitement. He missed his grandmother.

"You heard what your dad said," Diamond said pinching his cheek.

"Okay." Jailen ran up the stairs to straighten up the guestroom for Diamond. He had somehow turned it into a game room for himself.

"Thank you," she mouthed as she retraced Jailen's small footsteps.

"You happy now?"

"Yes, baby, thank you."

"I don't know why you're being so accommodating all of a sudden."

"I know that me and Diamond have had our issues, but that's all in the past now. I can't take away her right to be a mother to Jailen, and despite everything, her being there for him is what's most important."

"Who are you?" Jewel asked pulling Reagan closer to him as he softly placed a kiss on her lips, "I love you."

"I love you more."

$$$$$

"So what's the plan?" Pop asked as he sat back on Sacario's couch rolling a blunt.

"I mean I guess we just stay here til tomorrow, right?" Sacario asked.

"Well, if that's the case, I'll just meet up with you niggas tomorrow then. I'ma head to the house."

"You really think that's a good idea?"

From the moment Sacario laid his eyes on Kisino, he didn't trust anything about him, and after losing Will and Golden, he refused to let another one of his brothers die again. Sacario knew that Jewel was trying to keep Pop safe, so he was on the same mission.

"What you scared, nigga?" K-2 asked laughing, "We're not in the fucking witness protection program."

"What I look like? I'm just saying we gotta be focused, and I think we can do that better if we stick together, bruh."

"Yeah. Yeah. Yeah. Fuck all that. I say we ride out tonight," K-2 said getting amped up.

"Why would we do that?"

"Think about it. Kisino ain't the type of brotha to talk, right? What you think he gon' do when he gets Pop? Sit him down and slap him on the hand? Hell naw. This nigga is out for blood. Why would we give him that chance? We hit his ass up tonight, and we can be done with all this bullshit by the morning."

"Naw, I think we should just stick to the plan. You seen what happened last time, K. We can't chance it."

"What happened last time is you niggas were not ready. With me and Jewel both there, we gotta be more organized, right?"

"What you think, Pop?"

Pop sat back in a cloud of smoke and let the weed guide his mind. He was in a state of constant confusion. He didn't know where he fit in it all. He knew that Kisino wanted him dead, his cousin KP was dead because of him, he put Jewel and the M.A.C. Boys in jeopardy, but as much as he was tired, he couldn't just run away from the consequences of his mistakes. He owed it to his brothers to make the situation right. They all had their own problems. They didn't need Pop creating more.

"I mean I have to do whatever I have to do."

"It's set then," K-2 said jumping up, "Who wants to call Jewel and tell him the good news?"

Pop walked outside and sat on Sacario's stairs with a blunt in his mouth and his phone in his hand. He looked up at the deep dark sky and became lost. He knew he was putting himself in danger, but what other choice did he have? The love he carried for his team had to surpass all of his fears. He had a purpose even if he didn't understand it yet.

"Hello?" Jewel answered the phone groggily.

"You sleep, bruh?"

"Damn-near. Where you at?"

Sasha Ravae

"In the South posted at Sacario's."

"What ya'll doing?"

"Shit, but listen, I know that we're supposed to be handling this thing with Kisino tomorrow night..."

"What you having second thoughts? We don't have to do this, Pop."

"Naw, nothing like that. We just decided that we should ride out tonight."

"Who the fuck is we?"

"We, nigga. Me, K-2, and Sacario. Look, I know that shit seems janky, and we've been doing everything half-assed, but the time is now, bruh. I got us into this shit, so I gotta get us out."

"Not like this, Pop. Ya'll almost got shot the fuck up playing around with this nigga. Why do that again?"

"Tell me what is the difference between tonight and tomorrow?"

"Everything."

"Nothing but time, Jewel. You want to give this nigga extra time for what?"

"I know you think that all this is your fault, but it's really not. This comes from some shit that Kisino been had with Golden long before me or you. I'm just the one who has to pick up the pieces. I'm supposed to be leading ya'll, so let me do that. We'll handle it tomorrow."

"Jewel, this shit ends tonight. I know that you want to protect me, but you can't. I have to do this."

"Why?"

"I'm done with all this shit, bruh. I never thought I'd see the day when I said that, but that's where I'm at. I'm about to be 20, and I've been shot at more times than I can count. I almost lost my life the last time, and I don't know how many more chances I have left. I'ma always be a street nigga at heart, bruh, but I figure there has to be more to life than just this. I can't say that a nigga is about to square up and be a poindexter or anything like that, but I look at you and Reagan, and I want that. Well, eventually, you know? I mean my mama and daddy never gave a fuck about me. From a little kid until this very minute, I have raised myself. I don't want that to be the life that my kids will have to live. I see how you are with your family, and I just want something different. That's all."

Counterfeit *Dreams 3*

Jewel remained on the phone but said nothing. He knew the feeling of hopelessness that Pop felt all too well. Sometimes he wanted a way out, but he was stuck. Who would he be or what would he do if it wasn't for the street life he had been introduced to at such a young age? He didn't know how to exist without it. Jewel was the one who encouraged Pop to leave the money, guns, and drugs behind. How could he now be the one to selfishly perpetuate those things in Pop's life?

"I don't know what you want me to say," he finally spoke.

"I don't want you to say anything. Just meet us over here in like an hour. It's time."

"In a minute," Jewel said hanging up in defeat. There was nothing left he could say. He rushed around his empty bedroom hurrying to get dressed. He tried to be quiet, so he didn't wake up the rest of the house, but his urgency couldn't remain silent.

"What you doing up so late?" Diamond asked as she stood in the doorway.

"I got some stuff to handle."

"You leaving?"

"Yeah, just for a little while. I should be back before you and Jailen head to your mom's."

"When is all this gonna stop, Jewel?"

"What you mean?"

"How long are you about to hustle your life away? At almost 28, you have done extremely well for yourself despite the circumstances. You have two kids now who depend on you. What about them? What's gonna happen to them if God forbid something happens to you?"

"I know, I know, I know," Jewel said continuing to get dressed, "It seems like I've been hearing this shit all damn day."

"Well, maybe you should listen then."

"I've been hustling, slanging, whatever you wanna call it for almost half my life now. That's what I choose to do. Period."

"It's your life, Jewel. You're gonna do what you wanna do regardless, right? But we have a son. Do you want him following in daddy's footsteps? Stop being so fucking selfish."

"Bye, Diamond," he said running down the stairs.

Sasha Ravae

"You're not invincible, Jewel. Remember that," she yelled after him, but he was out the door before the last word left her lips.

Chapter 8

"Asaya, please be still," Veronica said as she attached the last wire to her honey-colored chest.

"Sorry, I'm just really anxious."

"Baby, you don't have to do this. We already have a warrant. I'm pretty sure if we searched his place, we would find something tying him to Roberts and Marcus Moore's murders."

"See, but I'm not sure you will. Kisino is smarter than that. What you think he has the gun politely laying somewhere?"

"I'm just saying, it's an option."

"Are we done yet?"

"Done."

"Okay, so after I get the confession, you will have everything you need to put him away for good, right?"

"If you can get Kisino to admit to murdering a cop, he will never see the light of day again," Veronica reassured Asaya.

"Good, I'll call you if I need anything," she said getting ready to leave the precinct.

"Wait a minute," Veronica said snatching her arm before she left, "I'm going with you. What if something happens?"

"What can possibly happen? My plan is to be in and out."

"Asaya, please stop being so fucking stupid. I'm coming with you, and that's that."

"Veronica, I've never snitched on nobody before. Let alone set them up on tape. I don't need the pressure of having my bitch outside with Sac PD plastered across her chest. That's not a good look for me."

"What if I'm not directly outside? What if I'm around the corner or something? I'm not sending you in there without any backup, Say."

"Do what you have to do, but please don't be all out in the open."

"I've been doing this a lot longer than you. Please just let me do my job." Asaya rolled her eyes as she headed for the exit. "Wait."

"What now?"

"We need a safe word," Veronica suggested.

"For what?"

"In case you need help."

Sasha Ravae

"Chase," Asaya said walking back toward Veronica's office, "I know you're nervous, baby, but I promise that everything is going to be okay. I'm going to be okay. You believe me?"

"What other choice do I have?"

"I love you," Asaya said kissing Veronica's lips. Her red lipstick coated her mouth as their embrace continued. "Nothing can take me away from you. You're stuck."

"Happily," she said smiling.

"See you in a minute," Asaya said as she sauntered out of the room.

Veronica sat back and let Asaya's taste linger. She felt like her heart had walked right out of her chest, and there was nothing she could do about it.

$$$$$

When Jewel got to Sacario's apartment, the sun was almost up. After he parked, he ran up the stairs that led to Sacario's front door. When he knocked K-2 quickly opened it up.

"What took you so long?" he asked closing the door behind them.

"I did just get woke up out my sleep, nigga, so what's up?" Jewel asked as he sat down. Sacario and Pop came out the back dressed in all black from head-to-toe matching with what K-2 had on.

"So I guess ya'll ready to go to war then, huh?"

"We didn't call you over here for no pow wow, nigga. It's time to put in that work."

"Pop, are you sure about this?"

"For the last time, I have to be, Jewel. If this nigga is asking for me and has been asking for me then as a man, I have to own up to that. I mean at this point, it's either I kill him or he kills me, and the second choice isn't an option. This is the only way I can get close to the nigga, so this is the only way I can make things right again. I owe it to you, Golden, and Will."

Jewel was loss for words. He always did well with direction, but leading the M.A.C. Boys on his own was hard because he didn't want to put any of his team in harm's way. He wanted to protect each of them. They were all valuable to him. How could he put their lives on the line as if they meant nothing especially Pop?

146

Counterfeit *Dreams 3*

"Jewel, I don't like this shit either, but what other choice do we have? We've given this nigga Kisino too much leeway. At this point, he's is reckless. It's time for us to take our city back."

How could Jewel argue with that?

$$$$$

After leaving the station, Asaya called Kisino and asked to meet with him. Reluctantly he agreed. She headed down Stockton Boulevard until she found the house Kisino had given her directions to. The dark two-story house seemed abandoned as it sat at the end of the block. As she stepped out of the car, she adjusted the oversized sweater she wore concealing the wires that were uncomfortably tapped down to her chest. When she got to the door, she knocked several times, but no answer. She waited and waited but still nothing. Asaya was convinced that Kisino had given her a dummy address, so in defeat, she headed back to her car.

"Ay," she heard someone yell behind her. When she turned around, Blue was standing outside with the door wide open.

"Sorry for coming over so late," she said as she walked inside, but he remained silent. Asaya followed him into the living room where Kisino and Dash were both posted.

"Sit down," Kisino said as he snorted a line of coke that sat on top of the glass table in front of him. White residue covered the surface. Dash had a liter of Hennessy in his hand and was taking it down by the mouthful.

"What's the occasion? Asaya asked wanting to break the ice.

"After tomorrow, the M.A.C. Boys will be no more, and I can finally get back to my regularly scheduled programming."

"Is that why you killed Detective Roberts? To get to Jewel?"

"That's an interesting question, Asaya, but I have a better one. Why are you here?"

"I want back in."

"Back in what?"

"This. GMB. I realize now that I was in my feelings behind Brandon's baby being born, but nonetheless, Jewel still killed my cousin, and I want him dead as much as you do."

Sasha Ravae

"Believe me, baby girl, that couldn't be further from the truth. Let me let you in on a little secret. Brandon meant absolutely nothing to me as do you. I gave him a simple task in an attempt to keep my lovely hands clean and your cousin fucked up the job. Now I have to waste my valuable time hunting these no-class having clowns down, so if you don't mind, your services will no longer be needed at this time."

"Come on, Kisino, I know I can help somehow. You may not have given a fuck about Brandon, but I did, and I still do. That's my blood regardless."

"Stand up," he instructed, and Asaya quickly did as she was told. The coke in his system clouded his vision, but he was certain that something wasn't right. "Is it cold outside?"

"Not really. Why you ask that?"

"I mean from all the times I've seen you, mami, you've had either your ass or titties out with no regard. I mean that is the uniform, right?" Asaya remained quiet. "Maybe I'm wrong, but I find it quite odd that you pop up over here at like four in the morning dressed like Betty Sue with that big-ass sweater on. Strip."

"It was late. I just threw this on," she stuttered, "I didn't know there was a dress code."

"Well, tonight there is, so either you can take off your clothes, or I can do it for you. You pick."

Asaya stood frozen in fear. She knew that if Kisino removed her shirt, she would be dead. Noticing her hesitation, he slowly walked up to her. "Shhhhh," he said placing his finger to her lips. He ripped the front of her shirt open exposing the intricate wiring that sat across her chest.

"Bad girl, Asaya," Kisino said shaking his head, "Haven't I been nothing but nice to you? And this is how you repay me? Just like your cousin, you're a disappointment that I can't afford."

Suddenly Blue walked up behind Asaya allowing his 6'8 frame to tower over her. Before she could turn around, he took her head in his hands and snapped her neck with ease. Dash sat back in amusement as her body dropped. Kisino ripped the wires from her flesh leaving her lifeless body still on the floor.

"Dash, help Blue clean this shit up," he said looking down pleased at partner's handiwork. He felt invincible, but with Asaya wearing a wire, he knew the police were too close for comfort.

Counterfeit *Dreams 3*

$$$$$

Veronica sat in an unmarked van with her newly assigned partner Derrick Watkins. He had been transferred to Sacramento, but his experience exceeded her own.

"So what's the plan?" he questioned.

"Asaya said she just wanted to be in and out without police interference," Veronica said with her earphones on. Although she promised Asaya that she would try to remain invisible, her safety was the only thing that mattered.

"Is that the smartest move?"

"Maybe not, but I have to trust her. She has more experience with these types of people than I do."

"But..."

"Be quiet," Veronica said as the conversation between Kisino and Asaya continued.

"Maybe I'm wrong, but I find it quite odd that you pop up over here at like four in the morning dressed like Betty Sue with that big-ass sweater on. Strip."

"It was late. I just threw this on. I didn't know there was a dress code."

"Well, tonight there is, so either you can take off your clothes, or I can do it for you. You pick. Shhhhh."

Suddenly, the sound of static filled the van.

"What happened?"

"The wires have been disconnected somehow. She said she would use the safe word. She didn't use the safe word," Veronica said beginning to panic.

"Maybe she moved a certain way and compromised the wiring."

"That's not possible. I arranged them so that no matter her position, they would remain intact. Something is wrong." She picked up her police radio and called in for back up. "This is Detective Matthews. I need back up to 7611 McTavish Circle now."

$$$$$

"You sure this is the spot?" Jewel questioned.

"It has to be. Kisino only has a couple traps in the city. I know he's smart enough not to go back to the Super 8, so my guess is that they came here."

"How do you know all this?" Sacario asked.

"My cousin KP, before he died, was moving up fast in the ranks. He got his work from here. Kisino trusted him with a lot, and being family," Pop said looking down, "That meant he trusted me with a lot too."

"I guess this is it then. You ready?"

"More ready than I have ever been," he admitted, "I know that this is what I have to do."

Jewel pulled out his cell phone to call Kisino. There was no turning back.

"Jewel, what do I owe the honor?" he sang into the phone.

"Listen, I'm outside on McTavish. I know that we said that we would handle this shit later tonight, but I'm ready to get this over with now."

"Aren't you a little eager beaver?"

"Fuck outta here. I'm not here for no games, nigga. I'm serious. You asked for Pop, right?"

Kisino was not pleased by the surprise, but the drugs in his system had him feeling like Tony Montana. He was ready for the world. "The door is open," he said hanging up.

"Okay, he's here. Me and Pop will go in and ya'll stay out here to make sure everything is cool."

"What I look like? Fuck that. I say we all go in. If anything looks suss, I'm shooting," K-2 admitted.

"We have to do this shit right."

"What's more right than us all going in together?"

Jewel didn't have time to argue. Time was of the essence. They all got out of the car and followed Jewel inside. "You ready?" he asked looking Pop in the eye.

"Yep."

"Everybody know where they're supposed to be?"

"Me and K-2 will keep a look out for big boy," Sacario said patting the gun tucked inside his waistband, "And whoever else wanna feel it."

Counterfeit *Dreams 3*

When they all walked inside, Kisino was sitting down alone on the couch. "What do I owe this surprise?" he asked lifting his head from the lines of coke he continued to snort.

"I'm a man of my word," Jewel said never taking his eyes off the gun that sat on the table next to Kisino.

"I'm here, nigga," Pop finally spoke up, "What's up?"

"Big talk from a dead man walking," Kisino laughed, "The funny thing about all this shit is I knew that even after the death of your own flesh and blood, you would run back to Jewel. This nigga has some type of voodoo spell over you, young blood, but you did good. I knew Jewel wouldn't be able to let you go, and you would lead him right to me. Now I can get rid of all you mothafuckas at once," Kisino said picking up his gun and pointing it at Jewel.

"You gon' have to kill me first," Pop said standing in front of Jewel. His trigger finger itched as he waited to leave Kisino leaking, but he couldn't afford anyone else getting hurt.

"No problem," Kisino said pointing his gun at Pop, "You will have to answer for KP's death in some way. Leaving your brain on the floor is enough for me, young blood."

"If anybody should be getting credit for sleeping KP it's me, nigga," K-2 said stepping up.

"Kisino, I don't think you wanna do this," Jewel said, "You're a slick fuck. I'll give you that, but did you think that I was going to turn my back on my brother? This shit ends now, so you have two choices. Either you and whoever you came with take your ass back to Texas, or your peoples will be coming to identify your body, bruh."

Suddenly the sound of police sirens could be heard in the background. With each passing moment, the whaling continued to get louder and louder.

"Not you too, Jewel," he said with disappointment in his voice, "I have to give it to you. If you can't beat them, join them, huh?" He wiped his nose as clear mucus began to flow. Using the police's inevitable presence as a distraction, he grabbed Pop from around his neck and pressed the tip of his gun into his temple.

"Shoot him" Pop yelled. He attempted to free his own gun, but Kisino's grip wouldn't allow it. Sacario kept his gun aimed at Kisino, but he hesitated to shoot because Pop was his shield.

"I think the police are outside," K-2 whispered.

"Jewel, look," Sacario said motioning toward the living room window.

Twenty police officers in all black stood outside as they all made their way toward the front door.

BAM. BAM. BAM.

"Sac PD. Open up."

"This makes it a little easier," Kisino said as he fired the gun shooting Pop in the head with no hesitation. His body slumped to the floor.

"Drop the gun," Veronica yelled as she and the other officers forced their way inside.

Hearing all of the commotion, Blue came from downstairs with a shot gun in hand. He fired three shots hitting two police officers, but in one swift motion, the rest of the squad proceeded to dump rounds into his body. He was dead before he hit the last step.

"Drop the gun," Veronica repeated, but Kisino continued to smirk as Pop's blood covered him. With no regard for his own safety, Jewel rushed over to him hoping he was able to defeat death one last time.

With no other choice, Veronica fired and hit Kisino in the chest with two slugs. He fell back into the table that sat behind him with his gun still in hand. Sacario and K-2 hit the floor not wanting to be next. Jewel held onto Pop's lifeless body in his arms as he watched his life escape him. When Brandon died, it hurt him to lose his friend, but Brandon happily made his choice. Jewel wanted more for Pop. He didn't want it to end like that. He was responsible for his death. He led Pop there to die. As he sat covered in blood, Veronica's heart broke, but once she realized it was Jewel, she knew she had to find Asaya.

"Matthews, I think you should come see this," an officer said from upstairs. Veronica rushed up the steps to find a body in one of the bedrooms wrapped in a white sheet.

"Please no," she said with tears in her eyes.

When the officer pulled the sheet back, Asaya's face was uncovered. Her neck was completely bruised from the break. Veronica felt like the wind had been knocked out of her. She couldn't breathe as she lay down next to Asaya's cold body. Her tears saturated her eyes until she could no longer see the deathly image.

Once the coroners came, they tried to pry Jewel away from Pop's dead body, but he was unresponsive. Jewel refused to leave his side.

Counterfeit *Dreams 3*

With no regard, an unsympathetic Watkins began to question Jewel, Sacario, and K-2.

"So how do you know the deceased?" he asked, but Jewel remained silent.

"They're brothers," Sacario chimed in.

"I'll get to you next, sir. Thank you, but I was talking to your friend here. Now what were you all doing here so early in the morning? There's cocaine and alcohol everywhere. Are those gun registered?"

Jewel continued to ignore the questions. He couldn't hear Watkins because he was so focused on watching Pop's body get bagged. When he heard the sound of the zipper close, he knew that Pop was never coming back, and it was all his fault. No matter how hard he tried, he was never able to escape death's destruction.

"This ends now," Veronica yelled as she descended the stairs, "Let them all go, Watkins."

"But I haven't completed our investigation. We have three dead bodies, Matthews."

"Four," Veronica struggled to say, "Now let them go."

Watkins didn't say anything else as he walked away to investigate the rest of the house.

"Jewel, I need you guys to get out of here, okay? I know how hard it must be for you to lose your friend, but he killed Asaya too. She's dead. Please just leave. I need you to leave."

Not needing to be told twice, Sacario and K-2 grabbed Jewel and left having to leave one of their own behind for good.

Epilogue

"Please bow your heads in prayer," the Reverend said as he began, "As we are gathered here today to celebrate a man whom we all loved so deeply, we also share the feeling of pain and loss. Words cannot describe the burden in which we all carry in our hearts, but our combined strength helps us to mourn our dear friend. Time passes so very quickly as we are all only here for such a short time. This is why memories are important to keep. The telling of stories and experiences with young Caseem will help us all feel his love as we celebrate his life. The time he spent here in the physical realm was the right amount of time God intended for him on his journey here on Earth. God, please heal our souls during this difficult time. Though we may not fully understand your reasoning, there are reasons for everything you do. Please keep Caseem in your arms and reassure him that pain will no longer be felt. He is now one of your angels who will rest in eternal peace as we all hope to do someday, so Caseem Carter, this is not a goodbye, but a see you next time. In Jesus' name we pray, Amen."

As Pop's body was lowered into the ground, Jewel, Reagan, Sacario, K-2, Gabrielle, and the rest of the M.A.C. Boys stood around his casket with roses in their hands. Tears quietly fell with every inch his body dropped.

"The family would like to thank you for your presence in honoring this young man's life. No reception will be held per their request, so please say your final goodbyes at this time."

Reagan tightly gripped Jewel's hand as the Reverend spoke. She knew he was broken, and there was nothing she could say to make things right this time.

"I'll be back," he said standing up. He was empty. He walked over to Sacario and K-2 who were standing in the back and pulled them aside.

"How you holding up, bruh?" Sacario asked noticing Jewel's lifeless expression.

I'm straight," he said not wanting to talk about Pop, "Listen, I know that before Golden passed the M.A.C. Boys to me, he was looking at you, Sacario, for who was gonna be up next. He made a mistake by choosing me. I want you to take over the M.A.C. Boys. I'm done with this shit, blood."

Counterfeit *Dreams 3*

"Jewel, what are you talking about? I know this is hard for you right now. It's hard for everyone, but don't you think that's a little drastic? What's the M.A.C. Boys without you?"

"Since I stepped up, mothafuckas have been dying all around me, and the people who I held closest to me are all gone. I wanted to believe that I was meant for this shit because Golden and Brandon spoke that life into me, but they were wrong. I did what Golden wanted me to do, and it worked, but to be responsible for the lives of my niggas, I failed ya'll. How can I live with the fact that Pop's dead because of me? I would have rather it'd been me."

"If that's the case then we're all responsible, Jewel. I hate to put it like this, but it was the young g's time. We all got one. Hating yourself isn't gonna bring him back."

"I kept Pop on this path, and it cost him his life. I have two sons to take care of now. I can't let them be raised into this shit. It has to be different for them. It has to be."

"So that's it?"

"That's it. I'm done. If you want this, Sacario, just say the word."

"I don't agree with it, but I respect your decision, Jewel. You're my nigga regardless of any of this street shit. That's not gonna change now. Sometimes I look at my lil mama, and I feel the same way you do. Like I could be that change and be something different than every other nigga I know, but then I remember that this lifestyle is what got me to this point. My daughter is able to go to private school cause Daddy can afford it now. She has a house to grow up in. She will never have to worry about where her next meal is coming from, bruh. I know this shit don't last. I know this system was set up for us to fail, but I wanna see me and my niggas rich forever, so I gotta take that chance while I got it. I guess it's my responsibility now."

To Be Continued...

BLACK EDEN PUBLICATIONS

www.SashaRavae.com

CPSIA information can be obtained at www.ICGtesting.com
Printed in the USA
LVOW10s2204081215

465959LV00022B/1285/P